ANNE DIGBY

Summer Camp at Trebizon

Illustrated by Gavin Rowe

DRAGON
Granada Publishing

Dragon Books
Granada Publishing Ltd
8 Grafton Street, London W1X 3LA

Published by Dragon Books 1982
Reprinted 1982, 1984

First published in Great Britain by
Granada Publishing Ltd 1982

Copyright © Anne Digby 1982
Illustrated by Gavin Rowe

ISBN 0-583-30515-6

Printed and bound in Great Britain by
Collins, Glasgow

Set in Plantin

For Lorna MacLeod

Summer Camp at
Trebizon

This is the seventh title in the Trebizon series.
You can read more about Rebecca Mason and
her friends in:

By the same author

Contents

1
End of Term

'Please shut up talking about the summer camp!'
Rebecca Mason said to her friends, the day before
school broke up. 'You know I can't stay on for it!'

It was the end of the summer term and their year in

7

the Third at Trebizon was drawing to a close. In September, after the summer holidays, the six of them would be going up into the Fourth Year.

As if missing the summer camp weren't bad enough, Rebecca had other problems, too.

Her friends had all picked their Fourth Year options and knew exactly what subjects they'd be doing for the next two years, in preparation for their big exams at the end of the Fifth.

Rebecca still couldn't make her mind up and secretly she felt a little bit resentful that her parents were always so far away. Most of the Third had been able to keep in close touch with home over this question of Fourth Year options. Her two best friends, Tish Anderson and Sue Murdoch, had got themselves all sorted out. Tish wanted to be a doctor, like her father, and he'd advised her what subjects to concentrate on. Sue had got in a muddle but then her mother had been down over the Commemoration weekend and talked to some of the staff.

It was around then that Rebecca began to feel at a disadvantage, especially now Pippa had gone. The girl who'd just left the Upper Sixth would have given her so much good advice. But it was no good thinking about that.

Even Robbie Anderson who might have been some help, was away on a French exchange.

Now term was almost over and Rebecca's parents were due home for two months.

Although she was longing to see them, that was a sore point, too. It was their fault she couldn't stay on for the summer camp! And there was the business of the dig in Mulberry Cove, as well . . .

Because they saw Rebecca so seldom her father and

mother had planned these summer holidays in some detail, starting with a fortnight's tour of Scotland as soon as school broke up.

Rebecca's five friends were all staying on at Trebizon to help with a children's summer camp. Every single one of them was being allowed to stay on, even Mara Leonodis, whose father never used to allow her to do anything at all. For Rebecca, of course, it was out of the question. The holiday in Scotland had been planned for ages. She'd been excited about it until all these other things had come up. Now it was slightly marred.

'Please don't talk about it!' she repeated.

Lessons were over for the day and the six were on their way down to Trebizon Bay, cutting through the little wood at the back of Juniper House that led directly on to the sand dunes. It was here in the copse that the tents were going to be pitched on Friday.

The school governors were lending the camp site to the Pegasus Trust, an organisation that ran holiday schemes for city children who wouldn't otherwise have a holiday. Some were from very poor homes and others were in care. All the voluntary help needed to run the camp and look after the children was being provided by the school. A lot of the Trebizon girls had volunteered, but there was only room for twenty. The five in Court House could hardly believe their luck when they were chosen.

They'd just been planning what games to organise for the children when Rebecca shut them up. Although Rebecca was really only teasing them they were overcome with remorse.

'Sorry!' said Tish in dismay.

'You know how much we're going to miss you, Rebecca!' wailed Elf — Sally Elphinstone.

'It's going to be rotten without you,' added Sue.

'Terrible!' echoed Margot Lawrence.

Mara said nothing. Although Rebecca was laughing by now the Greek girl knew better than anyone how she was feeling. Poor Rebecca!

They passed through the little gate marked PRIVATE TREBIZON SCHOOL that led directly on to Trebizon Bay. Rebecca and Tish ran on ahead and scrambled up to the top of the nearest sand dune. The huge bay was spread out in front of them with its great reaches of golden sand. The tide was a long way out today. Some little sailing boats, flashes of white on the green sea, were disappearing round the headland and into Mulberry Cove.

'When does Mrs Lazarus start her dig?' Rebecca suddenly asked Tish.

'Saturday, I think,' replied Tish.

'Do you think you'll be able to go and help, like she asked?'

'Only if we get any time off from the camp,' said Tish shiftily, trying to be casual.

'I think that sounds really interesting, I bet you'll go,' said Rebecca. 'And it *is* her last chance, after all.'

They'd all met Mrs Lottie Lazarus on the last Sunday in June. It had been Commemoration Day on the Saturday — a high point in Rebecca's life — and the Sunday had been Old Girls' day, when ex-Trebizonians of all ages descended. Sue's mother had been amongst them. In fine drizzle Rebecca had played in a School *v* Old Girls tennis match and School had been trounced. Afterwards, at Court House, they'd entertained to tea some old Trebizonians who were visiting their former boarding house, including an elderly, scholarly lady with twinkling blue eyes in a sun-bronzed face and a charismatic personality.

10

Mrs Lazarus was easily the oldest 'old girl' Rebecca had ever met at Trebizon and she was fascinated by her. She'd been a leading expert in Latin literature all her life, but for the past two years had turned to archaeology, trying to prove a theory that no-one really believed in. It was something to do with pirates in Roman times and a hoard of newly-minted Roman coins buried in Mulberry Cove, less than a mile from her old school.

'As soon as I read the text of the old poem, I knew it must be Mulberry Cove,' she told Rebecca, who had just brought her some sugar for her tea. 'I did no end of sailing round here at your age.'

She then quoted some very obscure Latin verse at Rebecca in order to convince her. 'You see!' Rebecca didn't understand a word, but it sounded rather mysterious and exciting. She had seen a bulldozer in Mulberry Cove one day, shifting boulders. Apparently Mrs Lazarus had brought excavation parties down before.

'We're having our last dig next month, so I need plenty of extra help,' said Mrs Lazarus who had taken a liking to Rebecca on sight. 'If you're staying on for this camp you and your friends can come over sometimes. You see — ' she looked unhappy for a moment '— the people who gave me the grant are getting impatient.'

'I — I'm not staying on,' Rebecca had said, with real regret. 'But I'm sure the others would like to help.'

Now as she stood on the sand dunes with Tish, gazing in the direction of Mulberry Cove, she was reminded of all this. She looked so wistful that Tish suddenly couldn't stand it any longer. She threw an arm round Rebecca's shoulders.

'I *wish* you could stay. Don't you sometimes wish parents had never been invented?'

11

When the cable arrived, that was just what Rebecca wished.

Rebecca put the summer camp out of her mind and on Thursday morning she packed her big trunk feeling happy and excited. Her parents' plane was due in at London Airport at mid-day. They were hiring a car for the holidays and driving straight down to Trebizon to collect her. They'd all night-stop at a motel somewhere and by tomorrow night they'd be in the hilly Scottish borders!

There they were going to spend the weekend in Langholm, a pretty border town on the River Esk, with Nanny MacDonald, Rebecca's grandmother on her mother's side. And it was Rebecca's fourteenth birthday on Sunday! It would be wonderful to spend it with her parents and her Scottish Nan, who made delicious home-made baps and shortbread and Dundee cake. Rebecca's mouth watered at the thought of it. After that they were going to tour the Scottish Highlands, before returning to Langholm for the colourful Common Ridings and then back to their little house in London for the rest of the holidays.

Not that she'd be seeing a lot of London these holidays. She was booked to play in various tennis competitions during August and her parents would be taking her around to them. It would be interesting staying in different places.

She packed her things carefully, taking a last look at the painting Pippa had given her before wrapping it up carefully and placing it between layers of clothes in her trunk. She liked it more every time she looked at it and had decided to give it to her parents. Perhaps they'd hang it up in their apartment in Saudi Arabia and the sight of Rebecca in her tennis clothes beneath the big

12

green cedar tree would remind them of England!

It was a hectic morning. All the beds in Court House were stripped and the rooms were being cleared out. The domestic staff was standing by ready to spring clean the building from top to bottom. Rebecca and her friends and the other Third Years across the corridor were giving up their ground floor rooms and would be moving up to the first floor when they came back in September. Tish had gone out for a last training run because she was being taken to the County Sports after dinner and had set her heart on winning the 800 metres this year. But the other five rushed round saying their good-byes and getting the school leavers' signatures in their autograph books.

The end of the summer term was always full of good-byes. The Upper Sixth were all leaving and had come back for end-of-term assembly. Rebecca saw Pippa all too briefly and said good-bye to Della Thomas and Kate Hissup as well. There would be a new Senior Prefect and Head of Games in September.

The six friends had done well enough in the summer exams to stay in the A stream and so were going up *en bloc* from III Alpha to IV Alpha. Rebecca and Sue went and thanked Miss Hort for putting up with them for a whole year.

The III Alpha form mistress looked stern and mannish but she was great fun underneath. She wagged her finger at Rebecca, although her eyes were twinkling.

'Now remember what I've told you Rebecca and think about doing physics. You're good at chemistry and biology and your maths has shot up. I'm sure you're going to be a science person in the end.'

'But Miss Heath says I'm an arts person and should get on with some Latin now,' protested Rebecca. 'And

13

they clash. I just don't know what to think!'

'Oh, yes, Latin,' said Miss Hort. She didn't look particularly approving. 'Well, you must sort it out with your parents. You're quite capable of doing either. Don't forget they're to write to Miss Welbeck in the holidays. Do you realise, Rebecca Mason, that you're the only girl left who hasn't sorted out her options?'

Rebecca grumbled to Sue about it afterwards.

'I wrote to my parents and they don't know any better than I do. I don't want to do physics – or Latin, either! I want to do home economics and scripture but they clash with chemistry and German and I like both of those. It's horrible having to choose, especially when they keep saying how important it is!'

'I know,' said Sue, sympathetically. 'It was a terrible headache fitting my O-level music in. I'm just glad my mother came down for Commem.'

'I'm longing to see Mum and Dad!' Rebecca said suddenly.

But when they got back to the boarding house, several girls came running out.

'Mrs Barry's been looking for you everywhere, Rebecca!' shouted Aba Amori.

'There's been a cable!' said Anne Finch. 'The postman came!'

'We wondered what the post van was doing here again!' added Jenny Brook-Hayes. They were all surrounding Rebecca. 'He's been once this morning.'

Mrs Barrington, the house mistress, looked out of a window.

'Can you come round to my sitting room, Rebecca?' she called.

Sue walked round with her to the Barringtons' front door at the side of the building. As the house mistress opened the door Rebecca stiffened a little and Sue gave

14

her arm a squeeze. 'In you go, Rebeck. Hope everything's all right.'

Mrs Barrington led the way through to the sitting room, waving a cable.

'I'm afraid there's quite an upset. I've just had an overseas phone call as well. Your mother's been trying to contact me all morning. I've got all the instructions.'

'Has the plane been delayed?' Rebecca asked quickly.

'Worse than that — sit down a minute, Rebecca — I'm afraid your parents can't get back to England for another two weeks.'

'Two weeks!' exclaimed Rebecca in dismay. She subsided into a small armchair. 'Why, what's happened?'

Gently Mrs Barrington explained that Mr and Mrs Mason were still in Saudi Arabia, having had the first part of their summer leave cancelled because of an emergency at a desert installation. Mr Mason was needed urgently to supervise repairs and Mrs Mason, who was a trained nurse and had been working for the company since January, was also needed because some men may have been injured.

'Two weeks,' repeated Rebecca glumly. No trip to Scotland, after all! No birthday with her parents! 'Then, I — I'm to go to my grandma's on the coach, I suppose?'

Rebecca's other grandmother, who lived in Gloucestershire, was her official guardian in England when her parents were out of the country.

'No.' Mrs Barrington consulted some notes she'd made on a pad. 'You're to leave your trunk here and your parents will collect it in a fortnight's time, after they've collected you. You're to go to Bath. I've got the address.'

'Bath?'

'Yes, to your Great Aunt Ivy. It's an easy journey and it seems she's your only relative down south who's sure to be at home. She's not on the phone but your mother's sent her a cable and presumably she's confirmed it because your mother says she'll be expecting you tonight.'

Rebecca's spirits sunk even further. Great Aunt Ivy! She was well-meaning but a terrible fusspot and rather deaf as well, so you had to speak in a kind of a shout all the time. She was Gran's sister, but a lot older. Dully Rebecca remembered that it was round about now that Gran was going to visit her two sons in Canada, Uncle Bill and Uncle David, so obviously that was why she couldn't go to Gloucestershire. At least she knew a few people up there. She didn't know anyone in Bath. It would just be her and Great Aunt Ivy for a fortnight.

'All right, Rebecca?' asked Mrs Barrington, kindly. 'I'll sort out a good train for you this afternoon and give you the time of the connection.'

'Thanks,' said Rebecca, trying to summon up a smile. 'I'll just pack a small case, then, and leave most of my stuff here in my trunk.'

She felt like crying with disappointment. She also felt a kind of rage against her parents! Tish's comment from the day before came back to her.

Mrs Barrington drove her to the station some time after lunch.

In Rebecca's suitcase were several little packages in brightly coloured wrappings – birthday presents from the others, for her to open on Sunday. She wondered what kind of birthday she was going to have.

Tish had gone off to the County Sports and Rebecca's last glimpse of the other four was of them helping to unload the Pegasus camping equipment at the back of Juniper House. It had been sent on to the school by

16

lorry in advance.

It was kind of the house mistress to take her to the train, because she and Mr Barrington were themselves about to dash away on holiday. She bought Rebecca's ticket to Bath and put her on the right train. Rebecca thanked her.

But as she settled into her seat and the train drew away from Trebizon station tears welled up and she ground her teeth with rage. Tish was right. *Why had parents ever been invented?*

When she got to Great Aunt Ivy's house in Bath that evening, it was even worse. She stood her suitcase on the doorstep and knocked and knocked. The sound echoed up and down the quiet street, but no-one came to the front door. Rebecca was rather taken aback. She knew her great aunt was hard of hearing, but surely she was expecting her?

She tried the door to see if it would open but it was firmly locked.

Then she noticed that all the windows were shut, some of them with curtains half-drawn across. She realised that she'd been wasting her time knocking.

There was nobody at home.

2

An Uncomfortable Feeling

Having managed to get into the back garden, Rebecca spent the night in her great aunt's greenhouse. There was nothing else for it. At least it was warm.

She stayed awake for a long time, waiting for the old

lady to come home. Darkness had fallen now but she thought that Great Aunt Ivy might be round at some old crony's house, gossiping and drinking tea. She kept watch, hoping and expecting to see some lights go on at the back of the house, signalling her return. But they never did.

So Rebecca moved some potted plants and stretched herself out on a wide, low shelf. She tried to go to sleep, but the shelf was dreadfully uncomfortable.

She slept very little until the early morning, when the sun came up and filtered through the walls of glass, cocooning her in a humid, heavy-scented warmth. She fell into a deep sleep and awoke with a start at about nine o'clock.

Rat-att-tatt-att-tatt.

Round at the front of the house, someone was insistently knocking at the door.

Rebecca got round to the front door just in time to see a red postal van disappearing down the quiet street. There was a slip of paper sticking out of the letter-box. She prised it out carefully and looked at it.

It was a docket explaining that the post office had been trying to deliver an overseas cable at this address, without success, and it now awaited collection at the main post office.

'It's the cable about me!' Rebecca realised. 'She's never received it.'

'Miss Mason's away,' said a voice suddenly.

Rebecca stuffed the docket in her jeans and spun round. A middle-aged lady was walking her dog past the house.

'Are you sure?' she asked disbelievingly. Great Aunt Ivy never went *anywhere*!

'What does it look like?' sniffed the passer-by and started to move on.

19

'Hey!' Rebecca hurried after her. 'Do you know when she's coming back?'

The neighbour stopped and looked Rebecca up and down.

'Three weeks, I heard. She's gone to Canada. It's none of my business, but that's what somebody told me. Her sister offered to pay her fare and she suddenly decided to go. That's what I heard. You'll have to call again another time.'

'Yes,' said Rebecca, dumbfounded. 'Yes, of course.'

As soon as the woman had passed round the corner out of sight she squeezed through the gap in the side fence, got back into the garden and recovered her small suitcase from the greenhouse. She just couldn't think what she was going to do.

'I'm starving hungry,' she thought.

Before she left the garden she helped herself to some ripe strawberries and a handful of raspberries. There were some early plums ready on a tree and she put half a dozen in her suitcase. She was sure Great Aunt Ivy wouldn't mind.

Then — perhaps it was the sight of her birthday presents that did it — she was seized by a horrible feeling of being alone in the world.

Her parents were far away and suddenly she couldn't remember what their faces looked like. Her room at Court House was stripped bare and empty — in fact it wasn't even her room any longer. The house in London was locked up. Of course, the summer camp was going on at Trebizon, but she wasn't supposed to be on it. There wouldn't be room for her there.

She didn't belong anywhere! She had nowhere to go!

She'd had the feeling once before when, as a tiny child, she'd got separated from her mother in a big crowd of people.

She sat on her suitcase in the deserted garden, trembling slightly, fighting down the feeling.

It soon subsided and she began to think sensibly again. She could telephone Nanny in Scotland . . . she could ring Claire or Amanda, her friends when she used to go to school in London . . . there were some kind people her grandmother knew in Gloucestershire . . .

Soon she was inside a public phone box and at the third attempt she got through to Nanny MacDonald, way up in the Scottish borders.

It was good to hear that firm, kind Scottish voice!

'What d'ye mean, ye silly girl, ye dinna ken what to do? Just go straight back to yon school. D'ye have the money for the train fare? Guid. Off ye go then. They'll look after ye a wee while longer.'

With a great lightening of the spirits, Rebecca retraced her route to the railway station and asked the ticket office for a single to Trebizon. She was glad she was still a half-fare!

Soon she was in the sunny train, with just enough money left to buy a hot cup of coffee. She sipped it slowly and watched the fields rushing by.

She was on her way back to Trebizon!

The feeling of being alone in the world had now completely gone. But while it had lasted it had been most uncomfortable. Now, sitting in the train, she forgot all about it. Later, she would remember it.

3

Together Again!

As Rebecca came round the side of Juniper House, she saw the brightly coloured tents dotted amongst the trees and heard a babble of voices. She smelt wood smoke and the delicious aroma of sizzling bacon and sausages.

Sausages!

It was twenty four hours since she'd eaten properly. With no money to pay for a taxi, or even to phone the school, she'd walked all the way from Trebizon station with her suitcase getting heavier every minute. She'd never felt so hungry in her life!

Now she dropped her case down on the ground and ran towards the camp site.

The summer camp was already in full swing. The children had all arrived safely, and the tents had been pitched. In a big grassy clearing, well away from the tents and only a few yards from the little gate that led on to the sand dunes, a huge brick barbecue had been constructed. It was from here that all the delicious smells were emanating.

A tall girl in a white Trebizon tee shirt was walking along the path ahead of her, holding by the hand a miniature edition of herself with frizzy hair and dark skin.

'Margot!' cried Rebecca.

Margot Lawrence spun round and stared.

'Rebecca!' she shrieked. She let go of the small girl's hand and rushed forward and hugged her. 'I'm dreaming!'

'You're not — you're not!' laughed Rebecca. Margot was cupping her hands to her mouth, yelling towards the barbecue. '*Rebecca's back!*'

Tish, helping to serve out hot food on to plates, nearly dropped a sausage in the fire. '*Where?*' she cried joyfully.

The little black girl did a cartwheel on the grass and ran off to join a group of small friends who were just finishing their lunch under a tree.

'Rebecca!' That was Sue. 'Mara, it's Rebecca!'

Then they were all jumping on her and thumping her

23

on the back — Tish, Sue, Margot and Mara. Elf didn't seem to be around. They were full of breathless questions —

'What's happened? What are you doing back?'

'Where've you *been*?'

'You look as though you've slept out all night!'

'I have!' said Rebecca.

'What *has* happened, Rebecca?' asked Mara looking at her worriedly with her soulful eyes. 'Has something terrible happened?'

'Yes, I'm starving!' exclaimed Rebecca. 'Food! Oh, Tish, are there any of those sausages left? *I must have food!*'

They found a plate, bread and butter, bacon and sausages and heaps of tomato sauce. Rebecca sat on a log and ate very fast and very hungrily. 'Oh, that's better!' she cried, crunching some bacon. In between mouthfuls she told them what had happened.

'You'll have to stay on the camp!' exclaimed Tish in delight.

'D'you think I'll be allowed?' asked Rebecca, wiping the remains of the sausage gravy and tomato sauce up with her last crust of bread. She'd cleared the plate in record time! 'I mean — the camp's full up!'

'Of course you'll be allowed!' they cried, almost in unison.

'Come on!' said Tish, pulling Rebecca to her feet. 'Let's go and see Miss Morgan —'

They started to steer her up the path through the copse, away from the camp and towards Juniper House.

'Hey!' called a voice. 'You — the girl with dark hair — you're supposed to be helping dish out —'

Tish turned round. A tall woman in a white overall, over by the barbecue, was signalling to her.

'It's all right, Miss Peabody!' It was Moyra Milton's

24

voice. 'I'll take over from Tish a minute.'

Laughing, the four friends continued to push and tug Rebecca along the path. 'Come *on*, what are you waiting for?'

'Who was that,' asked Rebecca, letting herself be tugged along and beginning to laugh with excitement herself by now, 'shouting at Tish?'

'Miss Peabody. She's in charge of the camp,' exclaimed Margot.

'Commander-in-chief,' added Sue.

'One of the head Social Workers from the Borough of somewhere or other,' said Tish. 'But never mind about her. Let's see Miss Morgan!'

Miss Morgan had permanent living quarters in the junior boarding house, a big red-brick building at the back of the main school buildings. It was known as Juniper House. She was the house mistress in charge of all the First and Second Years during term time. Although the rest of the school was now shut up for the holidays, part of Juniper House was being kept open so that the campers could use the wash facilities there, as well as the common rooms and kitchens if the weather turned very cold or wet. At the moment the weather was glorious.

She was taking joint responsibility for the smooth running of the camp with Miss Peabody from Social Services and was in charge of the twenty Trebizon girls who were acting as camp assistants.

'Do — do you think she'll let me stay?' asked Rebecca, suddenly overcome with fear and trepidation as the five of them walked into Juniper.

'She'll have to!' said Tish indignantly.

'I mean — well, on the camp? Do you think there'll be room? Do you think I'll be allowed to be a camp assistant?'

'Why don't we just find out,' said Sue quietly, with a touch of nerves herself.

But they needn't have worried.

As Rebecca told her story to Miss Morgan, the junior house mistress surveyed her thoughtfully. She was thinking back to her first meeting with Rebecca, two years before, on the London to Trebizon train — how dishevelled she'd looked, and how lost! Rebecca's appearance right now was rather reminiscent of that first meeting.

'So — please — I was wondering, can I stay on the camp with the others?' finished Rebecca anxiously, wondering what Miss Morgan was thinking about.

'I don't see why not,' said the house mistress. She surveyed Rebecca kindly. 'I'll get in touch with your parents and explain everything straight away so they know where to find you when they get back to England! I'm sure Miss Peabody can squeeze you in somehow. I'll come down and see her in a minute.'

She gave Rebecca a reassuring smile.

'We've got a fair number of homeless children out there already, you know. I think we can make room for one more.'

It was a lovely way of putting it.

'Thanks!' said Rebecca joyfully. She felt weak with relief. 'Oh, *thanks*, Miss Morgan!'

Whooping happily the five of them raced back to the camp.

'It's your birthday on Sunday!' Tish remembered. 'You'll be here for your birthday!'

Rebecca took a high running leap and caught hold of an over-hanging branch, swinging backwards and forwards in mid-air. 'I know!' she cried.

'Hey!' said Margot. 'Is that your case back there?'

Rebecca dropped down on to the grass and then ran

back up the path to get it.

It was great. They were all together again. But where was Elf?

Miss Peabody told Rebecca that she looked very scruffy, as indeed she did, and sent her back to Juniper House to have a shower and change into some regulation camp kit. Miss Morgan had a stock of it. All the Trebizon volunteers were wearing the same uniform – white school tee shirts and blue shorts – so that the young visitors could pick them out easily and get to know them.

Rebecca was greatly refreshed by her hot shower and hurried back to the camp, pleased to be in the proper gear. She was now, officially, a camp assistant!

She found that the other four had taken a party of children down to the sands to play rounders, but Miss Peabody wanted to see her to sort out some sleeping arrangements and to tell her the camp rules.

The previous night the Trebizon volunteers, having got all the tents pitched, ready for the children's arrival in the morning, had been able to sleep where they wanted. But tonight they'd each be allocated a tent containing two children.

'They're three-man tents, one assistant and two kids to a tent. Each assistant will be responsible for her two kids at night – see they get to bed at the proper time, don't wander off anywhere in the dark and so forth. These are city kids and most of them don't know the first thing about being outdoors.'

'So I'll have two children to look after, then?' Rebecca said with interest.

'Not exactly,' frowned Miss Peabody, checking down a long list with a pencil. 'You're not meant to be here, remember. You could come in my tent with me – '

Rebecca's heart almost stopped for a moment as the supervisor nodded towards a rather grand tent nearby. It was blue and almost square, with plastic windows, rather like a proper little house. It had at least two or three rooms inside, with simple furniture.

'– that's me, over there.'

'Yes?' prompted Rebecca, willing Miss Peabody to have a better suggestion.

'The only other possibility. . . . let me see . . . we've had a kid drop out. Marcus Roberts – he's gone down with chicken pox – so Tommy Carter will have a tent to himself. With one of your girls in charge of him, of course. He's a handful, is Tommy.'

'So I could go in the same tent – if the tents sleep three – I could help look after him!' said Rebecca, trying not to sound too eager.

The woman seemed slightly put out. But then she nodded.

'If you want,' she shrugged. 'It'll probably take two of you to keep Tommy in order. He's only eight, but he's got more nuisance value than the rest of the kids put together.' She consulted her list again. 'He's already decided who he wants in his tent. The plump one – Sally Elphinstone, isn't it?'

'Oh!' Rebecca hid her glee with great difficulty. 'Elf – I mean, Sally. She really loves children! I expect that's why Tommy's taken a liking to her.'

'Doubt it,' said Miss Peabody briskly. 'I expect she looks easy-going. That's what he'd take a liking to. Right, it's all settled them.'

'Where – where *is* Elf?' asked Rebecca, realising that she still hadn't seen her. 'The plump one. Is she with Tommy now?'

'Correct. All the early lunchers – that's the kids whose surnames come in the first half of the alphabet –

28

have been taken for a walk to Mulberry Cove. You'll meet Tommy soon enough. They should be back at any moment.'

'Is there anything you'd like me to do?' Rebecca asked politely.

Miss Peabody pointed to the camp fire where a group of Fifth Years were heating a cauldron of water, which had been filled from a nearby stand-pipe. A young man in a blue denim suit was laughing and chatting to them.

'Ask Donald. He's my assistant and sorts out everyone's jobs. He could probably use you on the washing up.'

So, up to her elbows in soapy water as she washed the dinner plates, Rebecca watched out eagerly for Elf and her party to arrive back. She was looking forward to meeting Tommy Carter!

But the party turned up, rather late. Tommy had given them the slip, it seemed, and they'd all got fed up with looking for him. Elf had gone back to Mulberry Cove, just in case he was hiding in one of the caves.

4

The Waif and the Stray

'He's a little menace,' complained Virginia Slade, who'd been one of the escorts on the walk. 'He was hanging round the bulldozer down there and pestering this man. When I called him back, he just swore at me.

Then when Elf went to find him, he'd disappeared.'

'He'll turn up,' said Miss Peabody philosophically.

'The rest of the children are such angels!' added Virginia. A small girl tugged at her arm. 'Yes, Sharon?'

'Please, miss, I got my shoes wet.'

Rebecca smiled as she stacked the last of the enamel plates and shook her arms dry in the sun. It looked as though she and Elf were going to have their hands full. But right now Tommy Carter and his misdeeds gave her an excuse to get to the beach. 'I'll go and help Elf find him!' she called across to Miss Peabody. 'He can't have gone far.'

The supervisor nodded and Rebecca shot off. She ran out through the little wicket gate and scrambled up the nearest sand dune, pausing at the top. Beyond, on the flat sands, an exciting game of rounders was in progress. A tall, skinny boy of ten had just skyed the ball and Tish, with an astonishing burst of speed, had raced across the beach and caught him out one-handed before crashing to the ground.

Everybody clapped, including Rebecca.

'Rebecca!' cried Sue, turning round and catching sight of her. 'Coming to join us?'

'Going round to Mulberry to find Elf!' shouted Rebecca exuberantly. 'How did Tish get on at the County Sports?'

'She won! Just over two minutes!'

'Wow!' gasped Rebecca.

Joyfully she ran down the steep side of the sand dune then cut across Trebizon Bay diagonally, away from the game of rounders, in the direction of the headland and Mulberry Cove. It was lovely to feel the breeze rushing into her face and hair and to smell the tang of the sea! There were some more sailing boats out today, she noticed.

She was thinking about Virginia Slade's mention of the bulldozer. It was back in the cove then — presumably clearing more boulders, ready for the Roman dig to start again tomorrow. The thought made her tingle a little with excitement.

'I wonder if Lottie and her party have arrived yet?' she thought, craning her neck as she ran round the end of the headland. She could just glimpse Mulberry Castle perched high up on a grassy hill, overlooking the cove. It belonged to the National Trust but apparently the tenants, the Willoughby family, always put Mrs Lazarus and Co. up when they came down to excavate the cove. According to Mrs Lazarus, the Willoughbys were great friends of her son, Charles. 'It must be fun staying in a castle!' Rebecca mused, as she gazed dreamily up at the old buildings. Suddenly she realized that her feet were getting wet.

It was easy to walk round to Mulberry Cove by way of the shore at low tide. But now, Rebecca realized, the tide was coming in. She bent down to take her shoes off, intending to paddle the rest of the way — and suddenly caught sight of somebody through a gap in the rocks, puffing and blowing as she clambered this way, a worried expression on her face.

'Elf!' she shrieked.

'Rebecca!' gasped Elf, her face lighting up with amazement.

They scrambled over the rocks towards each other and fell into a joyful hug. Elf was full of questions and exclamations and Rebecca quickly explained how she came to be back.

'Well I'll be blowed!' giggled Elf. 'And we're going to be in the same tent? Great!'

'Isn't it!' Rebecca agreed. 'We're both to be in charge

of this Tommy — er — Carter. Where is he, anyway — ?'
she looked around. 'You haven't found him?'

Elf shook her head. Together they climbed on to a big
flat rock and surveyed the cove. Several small sailing
dinghies were beached near a wooden hut, the head-
quarters of the Mulberry Cove Sailing School. Much
farther away, the bulldozer was just opening its giant
jaws and tipping a load of boulders on to a heap, clearing
a few more yards of beach. This was happening in the
lea of some rocky cliffs on the far side of the cove.

'You look worried,' said Rebecca. 'Miss Peabody
doesn't seem too worried about him. She seems used to
him. Do you think he's all right?'

'Oh, I'm sure he's all right,' replied Elf. 'I've just
been talking to the bulldozer man and he saw Tommy
just a few minutes ago. Apparently he was up on the
hillside there —' Elf pointed above their heads to the
gorse-covered headland that separated the cove from
Trebizon Bay, criss-crossed with little tracks. 'He was
running in and out of the undergrowth, playing with a
great big black mongrel dog.'

'Let's go back over the top then,' suggested Rebecca.
'We've got to anyway — unless we want to swim back in
our shorts! Look, the tide's coming in quite fast. We'll
probably see him on the way back to camp.'

They climbed up one of the steep tracks until they
were walking waist-high in gorse and sweet-smelling
grasses over the top of the headland. Trebizon Bay was
spread out in front of them with the deep bowl of
Mulberry Cove dropping away behind them. It was a
good vantage point.

'Can't see him,' said Elf.

'Don't look so worried,' said Rebecca.

'I'm sure he's all right,' repeated Elf, 'but I feel a bit

guilty. I mean, I was supposed to be keeping a close eye on him and I forgot. Not a very good start, is it?'

They were dropping down into Trebizon Bay now, passing close to a large wooden shack with *Cantoni's* painted on it. It was a summer beach shop, run by an Italian couple, that did a good trade in sweets, chocolates, beach equipment, postcards and ice cream. A lot of their holiday trade came from a caravan site that lay back some two hundred yards from this corner of the bay. There seemed to be more activity than usual going on around the shop, with a horde of people gathered. Mrs Cantoni was talking in a shrill voice. Ignoring all this, Rebecca and Elf walked briskly across the sands towards the camp.

'I expect Tommy's back, by now,' Elf sighed.

'We'll manage him!' Rebecca said confidently. 'There's the two of us now. We'll see he doesn't get into any trouble.'

But Tommy was in trouble already.

As the girls let themselves back in through the wicket gate, they saw that Mr Cantoni was there. He was holding a small boy with matted brown hair by the scruff of the neck, shouting angrily and volubly at Miss Peabody's assistant. The black dog was very much in evidence, frisking round the barbecue, sniffing and searching the ground for food. A crowd of young campers had gathered, all eyes and ears.

'I catch-a him in the act!' the Italian repeated. 'Right in the act! He try to hide one – two – three bars of chocolate inside his shirt. Is thief! Thief!'

Nervously Rebecca chewed at her thumbnail. So this was the famous Tommy Carter!

Donald spoke quietly, soothingly. Gradually the owner of the beach shop relaxed his hold and let go. Tommy

34

rubbed the back of his neck, glowering. 'That hurt, mister!'

'I do apologize, sir – won't happen again – ' Snatches of the social worker's talk came to their ears. 'This kid's very unsettled at the moment – just between foster homes –' Rebecca looked at the boy's guarded little face thoughtfully. 'No more trouble . . . I promise you . . .'

The Italian stormed off.

'It happen again I call the police. You keep-a these children under control, please.'

Donald chased the audience away and settled down on a log to give Tommy a talking to, the big black mongrel now sniffing round their feet and licking Tommy's skinny legs, affectionately, from time to time. Elf, feeling to some extent responsible for all this, hung around and Rebecca hung around with her.

'You've been a bad boy, Tommy.'

'The chocolate weren't for me, it were for Blackie!' The boy put his arms round the dog's neck and it licked his face. 'Look at him. They been starving him!'

The animal certainly looked rather neglected. He wouldn't have won a prize at Cruft's. However, that was no excuse for trying to steal chocolate for him, Donald explained – and he launched into a long, solemn discussion with the boy about being a member of a community and not letting the side down. In the middle of this Miss Peabody, who had just heard about Tommy getting into trouble, marched on to the scene.

'What's that filthy dog doing here, Tommy?' she asked, cutting her assistant off in mid-sentence.

'I found him!' said Tommy defensively. 'Can I keep him, Miss?'

'Of course you can't keep him, you stupid boy!' sighed Miss Peabody. 'Take him back this minute – I

35

don't know where you found him, but take him back there!'

'I i'nt goin' to,' said Tommy, his arms tightening round the dog possessively. 'He likes me.'

Miss Peabody turned to Elf and Rebecca, looking slightly weary.

'See he takes that dog back, will you? You'd better go with him.'

'Come on, Tommy,' said Elf.

The boy swore at her and shook his head stubbornly.

Elf started to walk down towards the gate, looking back at the dog.

She whistled.

'Come on, Blackie! Come on, boy!'

The dog leapt away from Tommy and went bounding after her. The boy looked crestfallen.

Rebecca took him by the hand and pulled him to his feet.

'Come on, Tommy,' she said gently. 'Where did you find him? You'd better show us.'

Resentfully, he allowed himself to be led out of the camp, kicking some stones along the path as he went. 'Oh all *right*, then. But he don't belong to nobody!' He didn't seem to mind too much Rebecca holding his hand. He glanced up at her.

He was a plain little boy, but he had appealing eyes.

'I've always wanted a dog of me own, miss.'

'It's funny you should say that,' said Rebecca, quite truthfully. 'So've I!'

Tommy had found the dog at the caravan site.

As soon as they arrived there, the animal bounded across to an empty caravan. The windows were closed and the door firmly locked. He pawed at the step and whined pitifully, looking up at the door hopefully, as though he expected it to open.

'What's the matter, Blackie?' asked Elf. 'There's nobody there.'

'His name's Nero, not Blackie,' said a voice.

A woman was sitting on the steps of the next-door caravan. She was covered in sun-tan oil, her hair was in curlers and she was reading a magazine. 'Jason!' she yelled at a two year old child who was hitting the side of the caravan with his spade. 'Stop doing that, Jason!'

'Is — is he yours then?' Rebecca asked politely. 'The dog, I mean.' Tommy had fallen into a sullen silence.

'No fear,' said the woman. 'He belonged to the lot in there — ' She nodded towards the empty caravan. 'They left this morning. Good riddance! Terrible noisy crowd they was — glad to see the back of them. But they just dumped the dog, didn't they? Wicked I call it.'

'Dumped him?' exclaimed Elf, shocked.

'That's right. Got fed up of him. Didn't want him no more. Cost too much to feed, I expect. Some people does that. Gets a puppy for the kids for Christmas and when it gets big they gets fed up of it and dumps it when they gets the chance.'

'But that's awful,' said Rebecca in dismay. Tommy's face was twitching. 'You mean Blackie doesn't belong to anybody. He's just a stray now —'

'That's right. I said to Harry we ought to ring the police.'

Tommy was holding on to Blackie fiercely now.

'It's all right,' Rebecca said quickly, exchanging looks with Elf. 'No need to worry. We'll take him on and see if we can sort something out —'

'Come on, Blackie!' whistled Elf.

The three of them left the site at a brisk walk, Blackie bounding along in front of them. Tommy's face had stopped twitching now — he looked bright and hopeful.

'Can we keep him at the camp then?' he begged. 'We oughter have a watchdog! You heard what she said, he don't belong to nobody.' The dog stopped in his tracks and ran back to them. He leapt up at Tommy, barking and licking his face and wagging his tail excitedly. The little boy laughed out loud. How different he looked when he laughed, thought Rebecca! 'See — he wants to stay with me. You and me are just the same, in't we boy —' He ruffled the dog's neck. 'You ain't got a family and nor have I! We could be good mates!'

Rebecca and Elf mouthed to each other over the top of Tommy's head.

'What d'you think? Shall we take him back to camp and ask?'

'Let's!'

They walked back over the sand dunes towards the camp. The tide was coming in fast now, long lines of shallow foam licking away the lines of the rounders pitch that Tish & Co. had carefully drawn in the sand, cleaning the great beach ready for another game, another day. A small sailing boat was disappearing round the headland, almost lost in a mist of green glinting spray, gulls wheeling and crying overhead.

Boy and dog ran down to the water's edge and back again, as though wanting to delay the return to camp. At last the small gate came in sight and Tommy said tensely, through gritted teeth:

'You *will* get round her, won't you?'

'We'll try,' said Rebecca, swallowing hard.

'Hadn't we better see if we can smarten Blackie up a bit first?' asked Elf nervously.

5
Tish Takes it Back

They made a kind of brush out of stems of marram grass, then crouched in the dunes and worked on Blackie's coat. While Elf held him steady, Rebecca groomed him with firm even strokes. Tommy danced from one foot to another and the dog pawed the ground and fidgeted, but it didn't take too long.

'There!' said Rebecca, standing up. 'Much better.'

'Come on, Blackie —' Elf clapped her hands. 'Walk boy.'

'Walk nicely!' commanded Rebecca. 'Show some decorum! There! Now you look a nice, tidy, well-behaved dog. Let's go and show you to Miss Peabody.'

They were so nervous, they started giggling.

They had every reason to be nervous, of course.

If it had been up to Miss Peabody, she'd never have allowed them to keep Blackie on the camp. Not if they'd brushed his coat for a thousand years.

But for once in his life, which had been rather an ill-starred one up to now, luck was on Tommy Carter's side. Even so, he had Rebecca to thank.

'What's the meaning of this?' said Miss Peabody by way of a friendly greeting. 'I thought I told you to get rid of that animal.'

'Please, Miss —' began Tommy, indignantly.

'Shut up, a minute,' butted in Elf and she proceeded to plead Blackie's case in heart-rending and eloquent terms. A crowd gathered round.

'Please let him stay!' said Tish.

'Go on!' chorused some of the children.

'He'll eat up all the scraps —' said Sue.

'Keep the camp tidy!' added Mara.

'He'll be a fantastic watchdog!' exclaimed Margot. 'Supposing we get burglars!'

Everybody started tittering and laughing, but Tommy remained white-faced with suspense.

Miss Peabody folded her arms and surveyed the dog with distaste.

'The whole idea's ridiculous —' she began.

'Rebecca!' called a voice.

40

To her amazement, Rebecca saw an entirely un-expected figure. The principal of Trebizon School was picking her way through the copse, stepping over some buckets and spades gingerly. Although she lived in the school grounds it was somehow surprising to see her down at the camp site.

'Miss Welbeck!' whispered somebody and the word spread, like a ripple, round all the Trebizon volunteers. Several of them, like Rebecca, at once began patting their hair into place and glancing anxiously at dirty fingernails.

'Rebecca!' the principal called again.

Rebecca hurriedly detached herself from the others and walked up the path to meet her. Miss Welbeck gave her an anxious smile.

'My poor child!' she exclaimed. 'Miss Morgan's told me all about it. I've just come to see if you're quite happy now.' She carried on past, looking with interest toward the assembled crowd. Rebecca fell into step beside her. 'I must meet some of the children while I'm here — is something exciting happening? But tell me, are you feeling quite settled now?'

'I'm fine,' said Rebecca, in surprise. It made her feel embarrassed somehow, a fuss being made.

'We couldn't have you homeless you know, Rebecca. Hallo —' as she walked into the clearing everybody stood aside and Miss Peabody turned to greet her with a rather ingratiating smile. But Miss Welbeck was look-ing at Blackie the dog. 'I see you've got a camp mascot!'

'Not at all, Miss Welbeck,' said the supervisor hastily. 'He doesn't belong here —'

Tommy's face twitched again and suddenly Rebecca blurted it out.

'He doesn't belong anywhere, Miss Welbeck! He really *is* homeless. The poor thing's just been dumped

41

by some people who were staying down on the caravan site. Tommy wants to keep him here, just for the camp —'

'I'd look after him, Miss!' pleaded Tommy, trying to be his most winsome.

'Now, now, Tommy, you know that's impossible,' interrupted Miss Peabody. 'We can't have stray dogs running around the camp —'

'We'd be responsible for him Miss Welbeck!' protested Rebecca. 'Me — and Elf — and Tommy —'

Everyone waited with bated breath. Blackie let out a long, low whine and fixed his eyes appealingly on Miss Welbeck, thumping his tail very slowly on the ground.

'What do you think, Miss Peabody?' asked the principal, lightly. 'Do you think the dog should be given a chance?'

It wasn't really a question at all. It was an instruction.

Miss Peabody opened her mouth and then closed it again. She glanced at Rebecca tight-lipped. Then she shrugged.

'Why not?' she replied politely. 'But of course if the dog's a nuisance he'll have to go.'

'Of course,' nodded Miss Welbeck.

The children cheered, crowding round Blackie and patting him, some rushing off to find him tit-bits. Tommy just stared at Rebecca, full of gratitude.

The six friends had some free time that evening so they walked over to Mulberry Cove to see if there was any sign of Mrs Lazarus yet. Tommy and Blackie had attached themselves, too.

'I'd like to drive that bulldozer!' said Tommy, as they wandered across the cove. It was standing idle now, work having finished for the day. Everything was quiet and Mrs Lazarus and her party obviously weren't going

42

to show up before morning. 'The way it was shifting all them rocks today!'

'Some hopes, Tommy!' said Tish. She was grinning and he grinned back.

'Why do these boulders have to be shifted anyway?' asked Mara.

'They're covering up the treasure,' said Tommy importantly.

He'd asked the man in charge of the bulldozer endless questions and was now very knowledgeable.

'The cliffs used to come right out as far as this — see?' He demonstrated, standing on top of a small boulder. 'They was full of tunnels and caves and they all capsided and fell down. Now all that's left of 'em is these rocks and humps and stuff on the beach. Mrs Whats-her-name says the treasure's buried under 'em all.'

'Why does Mrs Whats-her-name say that?' asked Rebecca, with a smile.

'This Roman bloke hid a pot o' gold in some caves. The first caves he came to, see? That'd be round about here, see? That's why she has to get the boulders and stuff cleared away.'

'What else did the bulldozer man tell you?' asked Sue. This was full of interest!

'Nothing much,' replied Tommy. He kicked a pebble, suddenly looking sullen. 'Just that the old lady's never found anything yet and ain't likely to. And her money's nearly all gone.'

He turned to Rebecca, hopefully.

'She will find something, won't she?'

'I don't know,' said Rebecca. 'But this is her last chance and we're going to help her look.'

'Me too,' said Tommy.

It was cosy in the tent. The three of them slept in a row,

43

Tommy in the middle. Blackie settled down at the foot of Tommy's sleeping bag, just by the open flap of the tent, listening out. It was comforting to have him there.

Elf was the first to fall asleep but Tommy seemed to want to talk.

'Have you got a Mum and Dad?'

'Yes,' said Rebecca. She paused. 'How about you?'

'Sort of. But they're a long way away.'

'So are mine,' said Rebecca. 'Where are yours?'

'Me mum ran off with someone and then me Dad ran off with someone else.'

'Oh,' said Rebecca.

There was a long silence.

'D'you see your Mum and Dad much?' asked Tommy, yawning.

'Not much,' said Rebecca.

'I don't never see mine at all,' said Tommy suddenly. Then he was silent for a long time.

That was when Rebecca remembered the uncomfortable feeling she'd had, alone in the garden that morning.

'Time to go to sleep, Tommy,' she said, reaching out a hand and ruffling his matted hair.

Blackie yawned and sighed softly. After a while they all fell asleep.

Next morning Rebecca and Tish took the two little girls from Tish's tent for a paddle before breakfast. Rebecca said:

'Honestly, Tish, we're so lucky, aren't we? To have parents, I mean.'

Tish nodded.

'And the things I've said! I take it all back.'

6
The Rock of the Lion

The weather seemed very settled. The forecast for the camp fortnight was good. Cold, wet weather could have ruined it but, if this first Saturday were anything to go by, they'd nothing to worry about. It was a warm day with a light breeze and plenty of sunshine.

'It's Rebecca's birthday, tomorrow!' Tish went around telling everyone.

'Then let's have a party and sing-song tomorrow evening!' suggested Moyra Milton. 'Can we Miss Peabody? I've got my clarinet in the locker in Juniper House — and you've got your violin here, haven't you, Sue?'

Sue nodded eagerly. 'We can play some folk songs — and plenty of other things.'

'As long as you don't keep the kids up all night,' said the supervisor. 'They'll be tired after their trip.'

They were going on a coach excursion to a nature park.

'Is it really your birthday tomorrow, miss?' asked Tommy, tugging at Rebecca's shorts.

'Yes. Don't look so bothered about it.' She laughed, feeling excited. 'I suppose you've forgotten to get me a present!'

It was only meant as a joke.

There was sailing that morning — and Rebecca was one of the lucky ones to go.

Sara Willis, who was head games teacher at Trebizon and lived in a cottage in the school grounds, arrived after breakfast. She'd arranged with the Mulberry Cove Sailing School for the oldest children on the camp to have some sailing instruction during their fortnight, on days when the sea was calm. The conditions were perfect this morning.

Miss Willis read out three names.

'Amanda Hancock, Rebecca Mason and Virginia Slade. I'll need you three.'

They'd all three done some sailing and obtained their R.Y.A. Elementary Certificates, Rebecca just recently.

They were to help the Sailing School instructors give the children some very basic dinghy sailing tuition in the cove.

'I'll look after Tommy this morning, then,' said Elf. 'We'll walk over to Mulberry with you and see if anything's happening on the dig yet.'

'Sue and I'll bring our four and come with you, Elf,' said Tish enthusiastically.

Margot and Mara were on washing-up duty, so stayed behind.

They all trooped over the headland with the sailing party, Blackie bringing up the rear. Up on top, Rebecca at once saw distant figures moving about on the far side of the cove, near where the bulldozer was parked. It looked as though Mrs Lazarus and her diggers had arrived and were making an early start.

'Something's happening at last', she said to Elf, as they descended steeply. 'I think that's Lottie over by the cliffs!'

They parted company outside the big sailing hut.

'See you lunch time,' said Tish. 'Tell you all about the dig, then.'

'Fine!' said Rebecca, sorting through a chest full of life jackets and handing one to the boy who was going to be in her boat. 'Try this one for size, Jamie.' She watched the others crossing the sand, Tommy and Blackie running on ahead.

'Be good, Tommy!' she called.

His voice carried back faintly on the breeze.

'They got a metal detector, Elf! Come'n!'

'Woof!' barked the dog.

Rebecca had a marvellous morning.

There was on-shore instruction to start with, the children being taught about booms, mainsails and jibsails and other parts of a sailing dinghy; followed by some knot-tying. Then, two or three to a boat, there came the practical business of getting under way from the beach, making sail and finally tacking backwards and forwards across the cove. There were eight boats out altogether.

'You're going really well, Jamie!' Rebecca said, when she let him have a turn at the tiller. 'You're picking it up much quicker than I did.'

Towards the end of the morning, a boat came alongside to starboard and one of the instructors leaned out, pointing ahead.

'We're taking a run to the island and back, to finish off with. You two are doing okay so you can follow us if you like! Just keep on my tail, Rebecca.'

'Thanks!' said Rebecca.

Although Mulberry Island, as it was called, was less than half a mile offshore, it was really exciting taking the sturdy sailing dinghy out of the sheltered cove and into the open sea.

The sea was calm today and the boat rose gently up and down on a low swell, into a frisky little breeze. 'Tack all the way out!' called the man in the boat in front. 'The wind's coming in off the sea. Coming back she'll give us a grand run in!'

As they made their way to the island, Rebecca talked to Jamie and found out more about him. He was one of the oldest children on the camp. This was his third holiday with the Pegasus Trust and he'd been looking forward to it since Easter. Although he wasn't in council care or even in a foster home, like most of the children, his mother was a widow and in poor health and there was no other way he could have a holiday.

'Except I did go on a school trip last summer,' he told Rebecca. 'That was good, too.'

They were close up to the island now.

'I wouldn't half like to get off and explore it!'

'Me, too!' said Rebecca.

Mulberry Island rose steep and sandy-banked out of the sea, covered in scrub and brambles and a few battered trees with a derelict cottage sitting in the middle — once the home of an artist. Rebecca and her friends firmly intended to investigate it one of these days, but so far had never had the chance.

'Okay! Turn about!' called the instructor.

With great care Rebecca brought the boat right round in a tight circle, as she'd been taught. This was the moment when it was easy to capsize! 'When I call out, duck under the boom and lean out to the other side, Jamie — and hold fast to the jib sheet . . .'

'Now!'

The boat had turned and suddenly the sails filled with air and they jerked forward.

'We're off!'

It was a straight, fast run back to the cove, running in front of the wind. Rebecca's hair blew over her face and she kept tight hold of the straining mainsheet as the mainsail billowed full out. Flecks of sparkling spume flew on to their shorts and orange life-jackets, quickly drying off in the sun.

'Isn't this lovely!' shouted Rebecca. 'Doesn't the cove look mysterious from here! Like a secret harbour!'

'And there's a lion guarding the entrance, miss. Look!'

'A lion?' said Rebecca in surprise.

The boy was pointing to a massive formation of brown rock that jutted out to sea on the left hand side of the cove. Rebecca had seen the big promontory many times before, but never from just this angle. Looked at face on, from out at sea, there was no doubt about it —

'You're right!' she exclaimed. 'It looks exactly like a huge lion — lying down.'

As they sailed on and a wave kicked up and showered her with spray, she thought with pleasure: 'A brown lion guarding the treasure of Mulberry Cove, down through the centuries. Isn't that romantic!'

Although Rebecca didn't know it at the time, it was the lion rock that had made Mrs Lazarus so certain she was right.

The cooked lunch, back at camp, tasted delicious.

'The dig's started!' Tish told Rebecca, through a mouthful of hot meat pie. 'Get *down* Blackie. Tommy, find this dog of yours some dinner, he's not having mine.'

'And guess what!' said Elf. 'Old Lottie says the six of us can come over tomorrow — all day — and help!'

'All day —?' said Rebecca. Then she remembered that the children were going off on a coach trip to the Battenbury Nature Park. The four Sixth Formers who were on the camp would be needed to help supervise them, but the rest of the Trebizon volunteers were having Sunday off. Rebecca would like to have seen the nature park, but this would be even better. What an interesting birthday she was going to have!

'Lottie's son is on the dig with her,' said Sue. 'He's Doctor Charles Lazarus — a doctor of science or geology or something. He's worked out all the cliff slippage and things in the last eighteen hundred years, to try and pinpoint exactly where the Roman hoard should be. He's really nice. So's his wife.' As she was speaking, Tommy nodded agreement.

'They don't half give you plenty of chocolate.' He frowned. 'But I ain't so sure about Mr Johnson.'

'What's wrong with him?' asked Tish, with a grin.

50

'At least he lent you his binoculars when you asked!'

'Oh, I dunno,' said Tommy. 'He don't think there's any treasure, for a start.' He shrugged and then gave Rebecca a sly grin. 'I spied on you in the boat wiv 'em. I saw you ever so clear. And the island. That looks a good place. It's gotter house on it.'

'I've always wanted some binoculars!' said Rebecca. She pretended to box Tommy's ears. 'Just think, if I'd had some this morning, I could have spied on *you* and watched you stuffing all that chocolate.'

Sue laughed. 'Rebecca, you missed nothing.'

The afternoon was busy.

The six organized and judged a sandcastle competition on the beach for all the young campers. Afterwards, as the tide came in, Margot and Rebecca supervized a group of children who wanted to go swimming while the other four went back to camp on Tea Duty.

But by evening their work was done for the day and the six friends lazed around outside Rebecca's tent, swigging canned drinks, while the Fifth Years took some of the youngest children up to Juniper for their nightly hot shower.

Tommy joined the six for a while, but when he realized they were talking about school he soon got bored and wandered off. Blackie meanwhile had settled down at the end of Tommy's sleeping bag, alternately dozing and watching them, through the open tent flap.

'It's funny to think we'll be going into the Fourth next term,' said Margot, lying on her front and sucking a stem of grass.

'I wonder if we'll get a good set of juniors coming up into Court House?' mused Tish.

They started enumerating which of next term's Third Year they'd like in their boarding house and which not.

51

'Have you thought any more about your options?' asked Mara, serious-eyed. Rebecca was sitting on the grass with her arms clasped round her knees, looking pensive.

'Not really,' said Rebecca. She'd been thinking about something quite different, not to do with school at all. There was an image in her mind. Suddenly she got to her feet and stretched.

'Won't be long,' she said.

'If I see Tommy, I'll see he gets to bed,' called Elf.

'Right!' said Rebecca.

She let herself out of the gate and into the sand dunes. She'd missed going to the dig with the others this morning. She had a sudden overwhelming desire to go over there now and get a look at the site — just a quick look, before dusk fell. They'd be digging there tomorrow.

She'd been thinking about the rock of the lion that must have stood on guard at the entrance to Mulberry Cove since Roman times, guarding the treasure — supposing there were any treasure. Anyway, that was the image in her mind and it sent a tingle down her spine.

Now, with an hour to go before sunset, it drew her back to the cove.

7
A Roman Riddle

It was silent and mysterious in Mulberry Cove. The
sailing boats were beached for the night and the shack
locked up. Over on the far side, the bulldozer had gone
and the site looked deserted. Work had finished for the

day. The only sounds Rebecca could hear were the screams of the gulls, the sucking and hissing of the tide on the turn and the quiet slip-slap of her own footsteps as she crossed the sand.

The sun was sinking over the sea. The shadows of the rocks and Rebecca's own shadow were lengthening.

High up on the grassy hillside above the rocky cliffs, Mulberry Castle looked down on the empty cove. Rebecca felt small and insignificant against such an impressive backdrop, a moving dot on the landscape.

When she reached the excavation site she stood half in the sunlight from the sea and half in the shadow of the cliffs.

She saw at once that the bulldozer's work had now been completed. An area about fifty yards square had been totally cleared of the half-buried rocks and boulders, the remains of cliff slippage over the centuries. The ground had been staked off and some trenches already dug that day.

Gazing all around, Rebecca saw that other areas had been similarly cleared and dug, evidence of past excavations. She remembered that this patch she saw now was to be Mrs Lazarus's last attempt.

She went down on her knees, just inside the staked area, and ran her fingers through the sand. She shivered with excitement. Romans could have trodden this very ground all those centuries ago, perhaps on a beautiful evening like this! She closed her eyes to imagine it.

Then she heard a voice coming from inside the cliffs.

It seemed to come from the nearest cave — a lilting echoing voice declaiming something in an ancient tongue. She got to her feet and stood there, transfixed by the eerie yet musical sentences as the voice grew gradually louder.

A figure walked out of the cave.

'Mrs Lazarus!' exclaimed Rebecca. 'Latin!'

The old woman stopped, and then laughed. Blinking a little as she got used to the light, she strode across. 'Do forgive me, my dear.' She recognised Rebecca from their first meeting. 'It's you. You've been able to stay on at school after all?'

'Yes!' laughed Rebecca.

They stood together in the silent cove. The sun was sinking fast now and their shadows were very long, moving imperceptibly on some nearby rocks.

'I like to come back here alone, sometimes,' said Mrs Lazarus. 'To see the cove as Cabro must have seen it. At sunset.'

'Did he write that poem?' asked Rebecca diffidently. 'Who was he exactly?'

'Cabro? His full name was Cabronius. N. Flavius Cabronius. He lived in the third century, A.D. He was a Roman, of course, and in command of one of the coastal patrols. Quite a hero!' Her eyes twinkled in her weatherbeaten face. 'At least, that's what they all say.'

'Who all say?'

'Oh, various scholars. Historians.' She spoke contemptuously. 'He was very zealous in the pursuit of pirates. Many's the time Roman vessels carrying cargo were raided by pirates – and many's the time Cabro pursued them and recovered their booty, then made sure it was returned to the proper quarters. At least, that's what they say!'

'And you don't believe it?' asked Rebecca, in fascination.

'Not a word of it. He was certainly very brave – but rather wicked, too. One can't help feeling a certain affection for him! He tackled the pirates with courage,

55

I'm sure. But all the best pickings he kept for himself. He must have been exceedingly wealthy!'

'How do you know all this?'

'Because when he was a very old man he wrote about his exploits. Some people who've read the texts say they're just a fanciful account of some of his adventures. But if you look a little deeper you'll see that this is an old man confessing his past misdeeds, not without humour. And proof of his misdeeds is hidden right here in this cove!'

Mrs Lazarus then explained that one of Cabro's achievements was the pursuit of a pirate ship to a point much further west than he had ever been before. It lead to the capture of all on board and the recovery of gold and silver coins, pillaged from a Roman vessel that was taking a consignment of newly-minted coins round the English coast to pay the army in the north. Cabro returned some of the coins – but not all of them. According to Mrs Lazarus, he kept a few of the precious gold ones for himself and hid them in Mulberry Cove!

'What – what makes you so sure?' asked Rebecca timidly. This was all so interesting!

'Well, what do you make of this sentence?' asked the old scholar. She spoke first in Latin and then translated.

Now in a cave in a distant cove lies the hero's prize, sleeping like the lion.

Rebecca's heart seemed to jump a bit.

'Can you say that again?'

Mrs Lazarus repeated it and then snorted. '*I* think it's quite conclusive but some people think I'm dotty. Dotty Lottie! They contend it's just a piece of poetic embellishment.'

Sleeping like the lion!

'The big rock!' exclaimed Rebecca excitedly. 'The one

round the headland there. It looks just like a lion lying down – '

'When you look at it face on, from out at sea, yes!' affirmed Mrs Lazarus. 'It's the kind of rock that would have weathered very little in 1800 years. The resemblance is still there, you do agree?'

'Oh, *yes*,' said Rebecca. She thought for a moment. 'And the *prize* is *sleeping* – like the lion. That means he never had the chance to come back and collect it. The coins are still here!'

'Exactly.' Mrs Lazarus seemed pleased with Rebecca.

Rebecca looked at the staked out ground that they'd be excavating the next day, with new excitement. 'So the coins could be somewhere very close to us!'

'Yes,' nodded the old lady. 'The caves that are exposed now, in the cliff there, would have been quite inaccessible in Cabro's day. Charles has assured me of that. The coins would have been hidden in caves in one of the sections of cliff that have collapsed and been swallowed up into the beach. We've covered some of those sections in previous digs. This is the next most likely . . .'

'It's also the last we can tackle,' she sighed. 'Everything's so expensive nowadays and the Roman Antiquities people are no longer convinced. They're only interested in the hoard, of course,' she added, slightly disdainfully. 'Almost certainly gold.'

Rebecca smiled in surprise. 'Aren't you?'

'Gold coins of the 3rd century A.D. are not entirely rare,' replied the woman. 'I have one in my own modest collection. It's what the coins *prove* that matters!' There was such a light in her eye now. 'I know that the history books are wrong about Cabro and I am right! And I want the world to believe me.'

57

The intensity communicated itself. To Mrs Lazarus a priceless hoard of gold meant nothing! Only the truth — that the obscure and long-forgotten Cabronius had been something of a rogue.

It only needed one Roman coin to be found on the beach at Mulberry, Rebecca realised as she walked back to camp, and Mrs Lottie Lazarus would be well on the way to proving her theory.

It was going to be exciting helping her to look!

'Thank goodness you're back!' whispered Elf, peering furtively out of the tent. Blackie was straining to welcome Rebecca and tried to leap up, but Elf held him back. 'Come in the tent a minute, quick.'

Rebecca crawled under the flap. It would soon be dusk.

'What's wrong?'

'Tommy's sneaked off somewhere! I haven't seen him since before you went off. Miss Peabody thinks all the children are down for the night — she's checking round the tents one by one. She says that any kid who doesn't go to sleep early tonight won't go on the trip tomorrow. Sue was reading hers a story and she told her to stop!'

Sue's tent was just next door.

'Oh, the little wretch!' whispered Rebecca. 'He'll be in hot water — and so will we. Have you looked to see if he's playing on the beach?'

'Every time I've tried to leave the tent, Blackie's tried to follow me!' said Elf, looking woebegone. 'Fat chance I'd have of sneaking Tommy back into camp after hours with Blackie rushing round and barking and telling everyone he's back! Now you're here, you can hold the dog in the tent for me! Where've you *been*, Rebecca?'

Suddenly they both froze as they heard a voice speaking softly at the next door tent.

'Boys asleep now, Sue?'

'I think so, Miss Peabody.'

Rebecca and Elf looked at each other aghast. 'She'll be here in a moment!' mouthed Elf.

'Quick!' whispered Rebecca. 'Unzip Tommy's sleeping bag –'

She got her arms round Blackie's rib cage.

'In you go, boy – quick – nice sleepies – in the sleeping bag –'

Blackie hesitated for a moment and then burrowed down inside the warm bag, while Elf quickly zipped it up over him. He wriggled and squirmed for a few seconds. Almost choking with suppressed laughter Rebecca patted and scolded him and said 'Shush!' Then she saw Miss Peabody's legs and feet appear outside the open tent flap.

'Hallo?'

As Blackie heard the supervisor's voice, he suddenly lay doggo inside the sleeping bag. Miss Peabody was bending down now, peering into the tent and flashing her torch on him.

'Tommy asleep?' she asked quietly.

Rebecca and Elf sat bolt upright on their sleeping bags, one each side of Tommy's, not daring to look her in the eye. In fact they were in such suspense that they hardly even dared breathe! *Please don't growl, Blackie!* Rebecca prayed.

The supervisor saw the hump in the sleeping bag and the regular movement of its breathing. She nodded her head, satisfied. 'Good night, Tommy,' she said and then withdrew.

As soon as Miss Peabody had gone, Blackie squirmed out of the sleeping bag and wagged his tail. Rebecca had to bury her face in his coat to muffle the sound of uncontrollable giggling. 'Good boy, Blackie!' she whispered. 'Good boy.'

'Oh, crikey,' snorted Elf, as soon as they'd both recovered, 'we really *will* have to get him in without being seen now, won't we?'

'The sooner the better!' groaned Rebecca, feeling horribly responsible. 'Leave it to me, Elf. I'll find him. You hang on to Blackie.'

As soon as the coast was clear she shot through the trees, making a detour to get round the camp unseen, then climbed over the fence and ran along the beach in the shelter of the dunes.

Several minutes later she saw a group of people walking towards her in the dusk.

'Tommy!' she called softly as soon as she saw him. 'What a relief!'

A man and woman were bringing him back to the camp. He was dancing along between them, holding their hands, as though he'd known them all his life. Rebecca rushed up.

'Tommy, *where* have you been?'

'It's all right, he's been up at the castle with us,' smiled the man. He introduced himself. It was Mrs Lazarus's son, Doctor Charles. He was with his wife, Antonia. 'We thought it might be his bed-time by now, so we've brought him back.'

'Uncle Charles and Aunty An showed me inside the castle!' Tommy informed Rebecca. 'I wanted to see innit!'

'Tommy —' Rebecca began, in some embarrassment. 'You mustn't call Doctor Lazarus —'

'It's all right!' interrupted Antonia Lazarus. She was a very gentle, delicate-looking woman. 'It was our idea. Down in the cove this morning. We feel as though we've known Tommy all our lives, don't we darling?' She

60

glanced at her husband and he glanced back at her, rather tenderly Rebecca thought. 'We invited Tommy to come and visit us at the castle some time.'

'We didn't expect him so soon,' laughed the doctor. 'Nor through the window!'

'*Tommy!*' said Rebecca.

'I seen the treasure, too!' smirked Tommy. 'I know what it's like now!'

Rebecca raised her eyebrows.

'My mother's got a few of her Roman bits with her,' Charles Lazarus explained. 'I showed him a coin much like the ones we're hoping to find on the dig. Coming to help us again soon Tommy?'

'You bet!'

'I'd better get him back now!' said Rebecca, taking hold of his hand. 'Come on, Tommy. Miss Peabody's been doing the rounds.'

'We shouldn't have kept him out so late,' said Antonia Lazarus, guiltily. Then, to Rebecca's surprise, Tommy let the lady kiss him goodnight. 'Night, Tommy. Enjoy the trip tomorrow.'

'Night, Aunty An.'

Rebecca dragged him back towards the camp site. He kept turning and waving to the couple, until they were out of sight. Then she bunked him over the fence. 'Come on! she whispered. 'And just you make sure you're not seen.'

Dusk was falling fast now and they made it to the tent, safely.

Blackie started to bark and bark with excitement and the three of them had great difficulty shutting him up.

They heard Miss Peabody coming across and Tommy quickly scrambled into his sleeping bag.

'Keep that dog quiet!' fumed the supervisor, not unreasonably, from outside the tent. 'He'll wake all the

61

kids up!' Blackie at once settled down quietly in his usual position at the foot of Tommy's sleeping bag. 'That's better,' said Miss Peabody. 'I'm warning you, if that dog's going to be a nuisance like this, he'll have to go.'

She departed.

Tommy went very silent. So much so that Rebecca and Elf exchanged anxious looks.

But he had something different on his mind.

'I ain't washed,' he said, at last. He yawned loudly. 'Or — or cleaned me teeth.'

'You'll have to do it in the morning!' said Rebecca.

'Hey, miss, wanna know something?' said the boy, very drowsy now. 'It's your birthday tomorrow!'

Rebecca smiled to herself. So it was!

'Better make sure you do wash then, Tommy!' laughed Elf. 'You can't have a dirty neck on Rebecca's birthday!'

As soon as the boy was fast asleep, they slipped out of the tent and joined the others round the embers of the dying camp fire. Dusk settled over Trebizon Bay and the moon rose, turning the sea to silver.

Rebecca told the other five all about the rock of the lion and Mrs Lazarus's Roman riddle. They exclaimed and talked about it for a while, before splitting up and going to their different tents for the night.

They were looking forward to tomorrow's dig more than ever now.

8
Three Birthday surprises

It was marvellous having a birthday at camp. There were three surprises in store for Rebecca.

The first surprise of the day was a dawn chorus!

It wasn't really dawn, in fact it was shortly before

breakfast. But Rebecca, still recovering perhaps from the night in her great aunt's greenhouse and the vast amount of fresh air and exercise she'd had since, slept late. She awoke to find herself alone in the tent, conscious of a great deal of movement and whispering and shuffling outside. Then suddenly, all around her tent, fifty voices burst forth in full chorus — some out of tune, some high and reedy: —

Happy Birthday to you
Happy birthday to you
Happy birthday Re-becc-a
Happy birthday to you!

Rebecca wriggled out of her sleeping bag and crawled across the tent, then opened the flap and peered outside. She laughed in delight. Apart from some Fifth Years who were on breakfast duty, and Miss Peabody herself, the entire camp appeared to be assembled there — even Donald! Sue, with her back to her, was standing conducting the choir. 'Encore!' shouted Margot, as she spotted Rebecca.

Happy birthday to you — They sang it through again and then all the children broke into loud cheers. Rebecca felt herself blushing with pleasure. What a lovely surprise!

'Bumps!' yelled Tish.

The next moment she was dragged out of the tent and lifted bodily — high in the air — down on the ground — fourteen times!

'And one for luck!'

'And one for luck!' they all roared.

'Mercy!' begged Rebecca.

She was left on the grass, exhausted and giggling, surrounded by her five friends. Somewhere in the distance the gong for breakfast had sounded and the children ran off sqealing and laughing.

'Come on, Rebeck, open our presents,' said Tish, helping Rebecca to sit up.

They all crammed into the tent while Rebecca took the brightly coloured packages from her small suitcase and opened them one by one. 'Talcum powder — thanks, Tish! Oh, Sue, felt tips — just what I want!' Then, as she unwrapped a silk headscarf from Athens with a picture of the Parthenon on it, 'Mara — it's lovely!' Finally, two paperback books from Margot and Elf. 'P.G. Wodehouse *and* Agatha Christie — hurray, I haven't read these!'

'Nor have we!'

'Mind you lend them to us!'

After that, Rebecca scrambled to get washed and dressed then hurried down to the camp fire to help serve out the last of the breakfasts. 'Remembered to wash your neck for my birthday, Tommy?' she teased him as she gave him a cup of tea. Embarrassed he averted his gaze and mumbled: 'Happy birthday, miss.' Rebecca was slightly puzzled by his embarrassment. He looked really scrubbed and clean this morning, so it couldn't have been that.

After breakfast, Rebecca and Elf were on sandwich duty and rushed up to Juniper House. There were mountains of sandwiches to be made for the children's excursion. They were going to be away all day. They'd have a picnic lunch at Battenbury Nature Park and then a picnic tea at Dennizon Point on the way back. The coach would be arriving for them in an hour.

As Rebecca walked into Juniper House she was met by Miss Morgan carrying a large parcel and a greetings cable. The cable was from her parents. It said HAPPY BIRTHDAY REBECCA PLEASE FORGIVE

TERRIBLE MUDDLE LONGING TO SEE YOU
LOVE MUM AND DAD.

The parcel was the second surprise of the day.

'It arrived at Trebizon station last night,' said Miss
Morgan. 'They phoned through and Hodson went
down to collect it — Red Star delivery by the look of it.
It's addressed to you, Rebecca — I was just coming
down to camp to find you.'

'Well, here I am!' laughed Rebecca in excitement.

'Many happy returns,' added the junior house mistress, with a smile, before hurrying off to find all the
things in the fridge that were needed for the sandwiches.

'Thanks!'

Rebecca and Elf put the big parcel on the floor and
knelt down, struggling to get the knots untied. 'It was
put on the train at Carlisle!' exclaimed Rebecca. 'Who
do I know in Carlisle —'

Then, as she drew out two enormous cake tins
covered in a tartan design:

'Of course, it's from Langholm! There's no railway
station there so Nanny must have got a 'bus all the way
to Carlisle — !'

The first tin contained the most mouth-watering
Dundee cake Rebecca had ever seen, rich and dark and
smothered with nuts. The second tin was crammed full
of home-made shortbread. And there was a beautiful
birthday card with a piece of heather and a note —

*If you can't come to me, then I must come to you! Happy
birthday, Rebecca, from Nanny XXX*

'Oh!' said Rebecca, quite overwhelmed. 'Oh, Elf,
aren't I lucky?'

Elf just nodded, staring mesmerised at the contents
of the tins.

Rebecca took a piece of shortbread.

'Try a bit, Elf.'

'My – my diet!' the plump girl protested, feebly.

'Never mind your diet!'

They sat on the floor and ate three pieces of short-bread each. It was very delicious and more-ish and melted in the mouth. 'Better put the lid back on,' sighed Rebecca, with an effort of will. 'We'll keep the rest for the party this evening. Mmm –'

She closed the tin of biscuits and hesitated a moment before shutting the other tin as well, taking a last look at the Dundee cake.

'– what a fantastic birthday cake! We'll take it with us to the cove – to have some with our lunch.'

'We'll need it!' agreed Elf. 'After all that digging!' She eyed it very solemnly and contemplatively, like an art connoisseur eyeing an Old Master. 'Rebecca, it's beautiful. It's going to be tragic in a way, cutting it.'

Rebecca laughed as they got to their feet. She was holding the tins in her arms now.

'I can live with a tragedy like that.'

A little shiver of pleasure ran through her. Today was doubly special. Not only was it her birthday. It was the day of the Roman dig!'

Wouldn't it be exciting if by lunch time, by the time they came to cut the cake, they had something else to celebrate? Maybe this morning they'd find some sign of the coins that had eluded Mrs Lazarus for so long!

It was a pleasant morning, but cloudy. In fact all the children were wearing their anoraks when they climbed on board the coach with their sandwiches. The forecast was showers inland. Blackie tried to follow Tommy on to the coach but Elf dragged him off. 'No, Blackie! You're coming with us today!'

The six waved the coach off from the back of Juniper

House then set off for Mulberry Cove with their own picnics, Blackie at their heels.

Rebecca noticed at once that the cove, so creepy and mysterious the previous evening, was back to its every-day self. There were a few people walking and bathing, one or two sailing boats being put to sea. Over in the lea of the cliffs the excavation party was working in the roped off area that the bulldozer had cleared for them.

When they got there, there were introductions all round. Mrs Lazarus was in charge, of course, holding an ancient metal detector. Then there were her son Charles and his wife Antonia, both wearing drill shorts, short-sleeved shirts and open sandals, busily sieving through piles of sand. There were two young men, stripped to the waist – Jake and Thomas – archaeology students from Cambridge University. Finally there was a wiry man in shorts and an open-necked shirt who had a small black beard.

'This is Mr Johnson,' said Mrs Lazarus. 'I think some of you met him yesterday. Did you meet them yesterday, Clifford?'

The man nodded. Rebecca gathered that he was the official representative on the dig of what Mrs Lazarus referred to as 'the Roman Antiquities people' – the organisation that had been funding all the work in Mulberry Cove for the past two years.

'Pleased you're here,' he said to the girls. 'Lot to do.'

He was right.

It was slow, painstaking work.

The men dug trenches to a considerable depth, the girls riddled and trowelled and delicately sieved through pile after pile of sand, eyes and ears alert for the tiniest glitter or the briefest clink of metal. Mrs Lazarus checked and cross-checked the rows they were working with the metal detector and occasionally it clicked into

68

life, only to reveal after much digging and sieving a rusty bottle top or a nail from a horseshoe perhaps. Once Rebecca squealed with excitement —

'A coin! I can see a coin!'

But it was a comparitively modern one, a big brown penny with Queen Victoria's head on it; an interesting enough find in itself, but hardly the real thing!

By mid-day, when the sun broke through the clouds, their Trebizon tee shirts were sticking to their backs.

They were glad when they broke for lunch. Rebecca cut slices of the Dundee cake and handed it round. 'Delicious!' pronounced everyone. 'Happy birthday, Rebecca!' said Antonia Lazarus, with that delicate shy smile of hers. She was a gentle, maternal kind of person, Rebecca thought. 'Will you be seeing your parents soon? I gather you don't see them very much.'

'How — how did you know that?' asked Rebecca in surprise.

'Tommy Carter told me.'

'Oh.' Rebecca thought about that for a moment. 'No, I don't see them often.' Then she smiled. 'But they're coming home on leave at the end of next week. They'll collect me when camp finishes.'

'That's when the dig finishes, too,' said the young Mrs Lazarus with a sigh. She gazed round the staked off area, most of it still untouched. 'For good. It's a race against time, really.'

They worked hard all afternoon, with no success.

But when Mrs Lazarus said her good-byes to them she didn't seem in the least bit downcast.

'Just look how much you've done!' she exclaimed. 'That's a whole day's work you've saved us! Now we can move on to the next strip tomorrow. Have you enjoyed it?'

They all responded enthusiastically and she asked

69

them to come again.

'Just whenever you can. Even an hour or two's useful. You all know how to do the work now.' She gazed out to sea, towards Mulberry Island, speaking in Latin. Then she laughed to herself. 'Oh, Cabro, what a job you've given me! But I shall win in the end.'

'Confident to the last, Lottie,' said Mr Johnson, at her shoulder.

'Of course I am, Clifford. And if you were half a man, so would you be!'

There was an edge to her voice and the girls turned away, embarrassed.

'Come on, Blackie!' Elf whistled. 'Time to go back to camp, boy. Supper!'

The dog had been playing in the shallows with a piece of driftwood, but came bounding up the beach as soon as he was called.

The six went back to camp over the headland.

'I really thought we might find something today!' sighed Rebecca, at last, the long grasses tickling her legs as they walked along a narrow track.

'We were all hopeful,' said Tish. She gave her wide grin. 'But I suppose it was a bit much to expect!'

'After two years, yes,' said Mara, dark and solemn eyed. 'That we should expect to be lucky!'

'It's hard work, isn't it?' said Elf. 'Must take a lot of patience, just to keep on and on. The way Lottie does.'

'She's just so sure she's right,' added Margot.

They all stopped at the crest of the headland and looked back – right across the bowl of the cove.

The party was now winding up the steep rough road on the other side that led to Mulberry Castle.

'Doctor Charles thinks his mother's right, too,' said Sue. 'I can tell.'

'So do I,' said Rebecca. 'I think she's right.'

70

They dropped down into Trebizon Bay.

'Mr Johnson doesn't though, does he?' said Tish suddenly. 'Tommy spotted it straight away.'

'Yes, he did, didn't he,' nodded Rebecca. 'I think Tommy Carter's pretty sharp.'

'You can say that again,' said Elf. She pretended to groan. 'I wonder what trouble he's got into today?'

'Let's hope a tiger hasn't eaten him up,' said Sue.

Tommy had had only an averagely troublesome day. He'd been in two fights. One with a small boy he'd met at the nature park and one on the coach coming home. He'd lost his anorak and then found it again. He'd sworn at Miss Peabody when she wouldn't let him have a second ice cream and been given a spanking. Apart from all that, the day had passed peacefully.

Just after the coach had deposited all the children back at the camp, he greeted Rebecca exuberantly. He was bright and smiling, as though a huge load had been lifted from his mind. He was obviously pleased to see Blackie again, who was barking and wagging his tail and jumping up at him. But it was more than that.

'Having a good birthday, miss?'

'Very!' said Rebecca, slightly surprised.

'Find any treasure?'

'Fraid not.'

But Tommy was still looking pleased with himself. He screwed up his nose.

'Mmm. Soup! Good eh?'

Rebecca was one of a group in charge of a big cauldron of oxtail soup on the camp fire.

'Have some.' She ladled it out into a bowl. 'There's some rolls over there.'

She was looking forward to her party that night. The others had discussed it with Miss Peabody and it had

71

finally been decided to make it a barbecue down on the beach. That way there'd be no danger of keeping the children awake after their long and tiring day. The next hour was spent giving the children their supper, then getting them washed and into bed. They were all ready for an early night – even Tommy.

'Guess what, miss,' said Tommy, as Rebecca zipped him into his sleeping bag.

'What, Tommy?' He was still looking incredibly pleased with himself and Rebecca couldn't think what it was all about.

'I got it now. Your present.'

'My – my present?'

He rummaged under his sleeping bag and pulled out his anorak, then took something out of the pocket, something that had been jammed in, wrapped in a crumpled paper bag.

'*Tommy*,' Rebecca swallowed hard. So this was why he'd been so embarrassed about her birthday, this morning! He'd been wanting to give her a present and –

'Sorry it's late, miss. The shop didn't have none yesterday, but I got 'em today instead. At the nature park!' He put the crumpled bag in her hands and eyed her expectantly. 'Open it!'

Rebecca pulled off the wrapping. It was the third surprise of the day.

They were very small and rather cheap looking. But, nonetheless –

'A pair of binoculars!' Rebecca exclaimed.

'They work, miss! They work really good! I saw the tigers wiv 'em – and an elephant!'

'And – and you paid for these, Tommy? With your pocket money?'

He nodded vigorously.

'Course I did, miss.' He could hear some of Rebecca's

72

friends coming. It was nearly time for her party. 'Don't tell no-one, will you?'

Rebecca nodded and put the binoculars safely under her sleeping bag. 'It's getting late now. I'll try them out in the morning. Oh, Tommy. You *shouldn't* have got me a present.' She was deeply touched. She bent over him and kissed him on the cheek. 'Night. Go to sleep.'

'Night, miss.' He was exhausted, but content. 'Was it a good surprise?'

'Just about the best of the day,' whispered Rebecca.

She had no idea then how much trouble it would lead to.

9

The Beginnings of a Guilty Conscience

Unhappily for Tommy, Rebecca found out about the binoculars the very next day.

The six friends were enjoying some off duty time before lunch. After a busy Monday morning playing beach games and swimming and paddling with the children, they were lazing on the grass outside Rebecca's tent. It was good to lie on their backs and to see clear blue skies again after yesterday's cloud. Rebecca noticed that her arms were getting brown.

'Wasn't it fun last night?' yawned Tish. 'You certainly had a good birthday, Rebeck.'

'Terrific!' agreed Rebecca.

They talked about the beach party. The two students from the dig had come. Jake had brought his guitar and played it and sung songs. Thomas had brought a local fisherman along with a haul of small tasty fish. They'd slowly grilled them all on the barbecue and then eaten them with great relish, under the stars. After that they'd cooked jacket potatoes and sung innumerable songs, with Sue and Moyra and Jake playing their instruments from time to time. They'd polished off the rest of the fruit cake and all of the shortbread as well, washed down with plenty of lemonade and apple juice.

Now they were all rather tired.

'I wouldn't mind a sleep,' giggled Sue.

'That's an unusual looking butterfly,' observed Rebecca, watching it alight on a nearby bush.

'Have a look at it through your binoculars,' suggested Elf.

Rebecca hadn't really been able to keep Tommy's present a secret from the rest of the six. She crawled into the tent but by the time she emerged with the binoculars the butterfly had fluttered away. So she idly focussed them on Tish's feet, instead.

'There's an ant crawling up your big toe,' she observed.

She swung them round towards the trees.

'Here comes Blackie. What's he been up to?'

Blackie came over to them, growling and snorting and waving his head about. There was a little rattling, clicking noise against his teeth. They all laughed.

'Oh, Blackie, not again!' exclaimed Mara.

The dog loved picking up small objects, twigs, buttons, small stones. He would carry them around in his mouth until he found somebody worthy to give them to. It was a bad habit because sometimes they got stuck in between his teeth and he couldn't get them out.

'Come on, Tish, you're the expert at this,' said Margot.

Gently Tish took hold of the dog's jaws, prised his mouth open so that his teeth were bared, then expertly extracted a tiny stone that was stuck between two of his teeth.

'You silly animal!' she laughed, then flicked the stone away.

'Woof!' said Blackie gratefully.

They continued to sprawl and chatter, Rebecca idly sweeping her binoculars backwards and forwards across the surrounding scenery.

'What date reads the same upside down as the right way up?' asked Elf.

'Oh, Elf,' protested Mara. 'My brain's on holiday.'

There were the inevitable comments and wisecracks about that — 'What brain?' — 'Isn't it too small to go on holiday?' — and so on.

But Tish frowned in concentration.

'The first of January, 1911,' she suggested.

'Eh?' said Elf. 'How come?'

'Well — 1.1.11, of course,' said Tish.

'No!' replied Elf. 'The answer's 1961.'

They argued about it for a while.

'All right then,' said Tish, deciding to get her own back. 'What's the longest living animal — vertebrate that is —'

'Elephant?' asked Margot.

But Rebecca knew the answer to that.

'Tortoise!'

'Correct,' said Tish. Then, seeing one of her small girls approach: 'What's the matter, Janine?'

The little girl was pointing to the binoculars in Rebecca's hand.

'Ooh, Tishy. She shouldn't have those! They belong to the nature park. You're only s'posed to borrer them!'

The six exchanged startled glances.

'How do you mean?' Rebecca asked the little girl, gently.

'Well, you put 10p in a slot see? — and get them out to look at the animals, but then you're s'posed to put them back.' Her eyes grew round with interest. 'Did Tommy Carter *pinch* them, miss?'

Rebecca rammed the small binoculars in the pocket of her shorts and got to her feet.

'I think I'll go and find Tommy,' she said.

Blackie followed her.

The other five surrounded the little girl.

'Now don't you go spreading this around, Janine. Promise?'

'D'you think he did pinch them?' she repeated.

'You just leave it to us, Janine. We'll get it sorted out.'

Rebecca ran out of the little gate, up and over the sand dunes. A game of beach cricket had just finished and Donald was blowing a whistle to call the children in. Blackie was the first to spot Tommy. He was in the far distance, down by the shore, ignoring the whistle and idly skimming stones on the water.

Blackie streaked across the sands. Rebecca took it at a walk.

77

'Hallo, Tommy,' she said, coming up behind him. He'd thrown a stick in the water for Blackie and the dog was gamely chasing it as it bobbed on the little waves.

'Oh, hiya,' he said, grinning with pleasure as he turned round and saw Rebecca.

He didn't grin for long.

'I thought you said you paid for these, Tommy,' she said, taking the binoculars out of her pocket. 'With your pocket money.'

He scowled.

'I did . . . well, sort of. It *was* me pocket money.'

'What was your pocket money, Tommy?'

Silence.

'The ten pence you put in the slot?'

He nodded, slowly, looking down at the ground.

'But that was just to hire them, wasn't it, Tommy? You were supposed to lock them back in their case, after you'd finished with them. Ready for the next person to come along and put ten pence in. Lots of people want to hire binoculars to watch the wild animals.'

He shrugged, still refusing to meet her eye.

'There were loads of pairs.'

'But there wouldn't be any at all if everyone did what you did, would there?'

He set his lips sullenly. Rebecca could feel spots of colour burning in her cheeks. She was furious with him — and furious with herself for accepting the gift without really thinking about the cost, even of a cheap pair of binoculars like these. She swallowed hard.

'Put your hand out.'

Automatically he obeyed and she placed the binoculars in his hand.

'Have them back, Tommy. I don't want them. Maybe sometime you'd like to send them back where they belong. I don't want anything to do with them. I don't want to know.'

She turned on her heel. She heard him curse. She turned back and looked at him.

'I don't like you when you steal. I don't like you when you tell lies. And I don't like you when you swear. I like you the rest of the time. In f-fact, Tommy,' her voice tripped slightly, 'the rest of the time I actually like you a lot.'

Her last glimpse of him was a small silhouette, standing down by the shore, Blackie beside him. He had the binoculars in his hand and she had the feeling he might have been crying.

As she walked across the sands she thought she heard the distant sound of a splash, behind her, as though he'd thrown something in the sea. Donald passed close by her, blowing his whistle. 'Come on, Tommy. Lunch time. Come on — *are you deaf*?'

She forced herself not to look back and returned to camp.

Tommy went and sat in the tent for a while after lunch and Elf found him there, sitting in the shadows.

'Look, Tommy, Rebecca's told me a bit about it. I've been and got brown paper and string from Miss Morgan. We can make a parcel of them. I'll help you. I'll help you write the address and then we can get some stamps —'

'I chucked them away,' said Tommy sullenly. 'I chucked them in the sea. I bet they're miles away by now.'

'Oh,' said Elf.

But not long after she'd left the tent, Blackie came bounding in. He deposited something at Tommy's feet and barked and wagged his tail.

Tommy found himself staring at the binoculars, which were wet and sandy and had seaweed sticking to them.

'I don't want 'em, Blackie!' he said furiously.

They lay there, lenses uppermost, like a pair of eyes reproaching him. Guiltily, he looked around the tent. Then he snatched up his anorak, stuffed the binoculars into the pocket and then bundled the anorak under his sleeping bag.

'I'll just forget about 'em now,' he thought fiercely. 'Forget all about it.'

But it wasn't going to be as easy as that.

10
Rebecca's Exciting Discovery

As far as the six were concerned, the binoculars had been washed away to sea. So that was that.

There was nothing Rebecca could do about it so she put it out of her mind. She'd no idea that they were, in fact, hidden in the tent. Tommy made sure that she never found out.

As far as Tommy was concerned, he tried to put the binoculars out of *his* mind, too. But sometimes, tidying up the tent in the morning, or wearing his anorak on cool evenings, he would feel the hard knobble in the pocket and feel guilty. He disliked this feeling very much, this prick of conscience, and would try to banish it as quickly as possible. He couldn't actually bring himself to do anything about it.

It wasn't as though he wanted to keep the binoculars for himself. He was beginning to hate them. Their presence in the tent was an embarrassment, coming between him and Rebecca somehow. He'd have liked to have gone and thrown them in the sea again, but his conscience wouldn't let him do that now, either.

So, in spite of the many happy days that followed, there was a kind of small barrier between Tommy and Rebecca and it was all on Tommy's side.

'I don't think he's ever really forgiven me for handing his present back to him,' she said to Tish one day. 'But I had to, didn't I?'

Tish nodded. She looked thoughtful.

'I'm not sure it's that. He looks guilty when he sees you sometimes. Whatever you said to him, I think it made an impression on him. He's much better behaved. I haven't heard him swear for days.'

'Oh, I'm sure that's *Uncle Charlie* and *Aunty An's* influence!' smiled Rebecca. 'Not mine.'

One of the most surprising aspects of the summer camp was the way that Tommy Carter, such a plain little boy and entirely lacking in good manners, had appealed instantly to Doctor Charles Lazarus and his wife, who were, to put it mildly, a very well-bred couple. With

82

Miss Peabody's permission he was spending more and more time in their company, together with Blackie, and was even making himself useful on the dig. To Rebecca's chagrin, because the six had regular camp chores to do, he was able to keep more closely in touch with events at Mulberry Cove than any of them and often she had to ask him for the latest news. However the exciting discovery was going to be Rebecca's alone.

Two people who weren't too surprised about the unlikely relationship between Tommy and the Lazaruses were Miss Peabody and her assistant Donald. They knew the reason and being experienced case workers they'd seen this sort of thing before.

'I think we're taking a risk, Sheila,' Donald said to Miss Peabody one day. 'Antonia Lazarus makes no bones about it. Little Carter reminds her of the son she lost — Paul, wasn't it — and it's all getting a bit intense. Tommy's a substitute. When she looks at him she's not really seeing Tommy Carter at all but her own son, Paul Lazarus.'

'Well?' said Miss Peabody. She glowered.

'Don't you think . . .' Donald hesitated, then decided to stick to his guns. 'Tommy's behaving so far. Enjoying all the attention. But sooner or later he'll start playing them up. He always does. It'll hit them — bingo. He's not Paul Lazarus whose name was down for Eton and all that. He's a little nuisance called Tommy Carter. And if they reject him —'

'I think they've got more sense than you give them credit for,' Miss Peabody cut in.

'Yes, but it *is* a risk —'

'Tommy's at risk anyway. He's sharp as a needle and full of cunning. If he doesn't get a family of his own and some love and discipline soon, he'll go the way his type always does. Petty crime, then juvenile court, then Borstal. Get your head out of the text books, Donald. Tommy Carter needs a good home . . .'

She brought the discussion abruptly to a close.

' . . . this friendship with the Lazaruses just might lead somewhere.'

Rebecca wasn't worried about Tommy. True, there was the occasional friction between the boy and Miss Peabody over Blackie – especially one day when Blackie pulled one of the tents down. The supervisor's dislike of having the dog on the camp was deep-seated. But that apart, Tommy was probably having the happiest fortnight of his life.

But Rebecca began to get worried about Mrs Lazarus.

They went over and helped with the dig whenever they could and on the second Sunday she, Tish and Sue spent the whole afternoon there. The other three were needed to supervise Under-10 swimming in the school sports centre's indoor pool. It had turned rough in Trebizon Bay with big breakers – perfect for surfing but not for small swimmers.

The three girls threw themselves into the work as enthusiastically as ever, working along the trenches on hands and knees, raking and trowelling and sieving the piles of sand and spoil. It had been misty the previous night and today the weather was humid and thundery. Rebecca and her two best friends, coming to Mulberry Cove fresh after a break of two days, were as hopeful as ever – always expectant that today might be the lucky day.

But amongst the full-time diggers, tempers were wearing a little thin: the weather didn't help. Of the area that had been staked off, some two thirds had now been covered.

'Another four days should see the back of this job,' Mr Johnson said to the students at one point. 'I expect you'll be glad to get home.'

Rebecca saw a flash of annoyance cross Mrs Lazarus's face.

'You make it quite obvious that *you* will be, Clifford.'

'I think Clifford is now convinced that he'll be going back to the Midlands empty-handed, mother,' said Charles Lazarus, drily. 'That your theory is far-fetched, that my calculations are highly suspect and the whole project — in short — has been a waste of their valuable resources.'

He spoke lightly, but the strain showed on his face.

After the three friends had left the cove, they stood on top of the headland for a while. Sue said:

'Lottie seemed different today, didn't she? Much older, somehow.'

Tish nodded.

'It's as if, for the first time, the unthinkable's occurred to her. That she may have to concede defeat. That no-one's ever going to believe it's true what she says about Cabro.'

Rebecca was silent. She was looking down into the cove. Thin layers of summer mist were drifting in from the sea, giving it that eerie, uninhabited look again. She'd been out sailing three times since Jamie had first pointed out the rock of the lion. Each time it had looked more real, more lion-like. *Now in a cave in a distant cove lies the hero's prize, sleeping like the lion*. The words that N. Flavius Cabronius had once written sent a tingle down her spine, each time she remembered them. And she remembered them now.

'Please let Lottie find something,' she thought.

Aloud she said:

'It was hard work, wasn't it? I feel hot and sticky all over.'

Tish turned away from the cove, and looked in the Trebizon Bay direction. It was free of mist. 'Look!' she cried, flinging an arm out. 'Harry's down there — he might let us do some surfing!'

A few minutes later, joined by Elf and Margot, they were riding the big breakers in the bay on the school Malibu boards, shrieking with pleasure as the cool salty spray drenched them from head to toe, the hothouse atmosphere of Mulberry Cove forgotten.

It was Rebecca who made the exciting discovery, on the Wednesday morning.

Tommy, who'd spent the Tuesday afternoon in the cove with the Lazaruses, had come back at tea-time and told them about the squabble. He was more subdued than Rebecca had ever seen him; obviously it had made a deep impression on him.

'Mr Johnson says it's all Uncle Charlie's fault they ain't found anything. Uncle Charlie's ever so upset an' so's Auntie An.'

'Have a jam sandwich, Tommy,' said Tish. 'And do cheer up. People say things they don't mean when they're fed up and tired out. It's all been going on so long . . .'

'Now it's nearly over,' sighed Elf.

Later Rebecca said to her friends: 'Isn't it sad if it's all going to end like this? Recriminations . . . squabbles.' How must Mrs Lazarus be feeling! Suddenly she added: 'Let's go down there in the morning! We're free after breakfast. All the children are going on the boat trip!'

'But only till eleven o'clock,' said Margot dubiously. 'We're supposed to stay around camp — hot drinks to get ready —'

'There's still time!' said Rebecca. 'Even if it's only for an hour, it's still worth it!'

So on Wednesday morning the six waved the children off on their pleasure boat trip to Mulberry Island, before going to the cove, accompanied by Blackie. Tommy had wanted to take the dog on the boat trip but Miss Peabody had said no.

'Hallo, girls!' Mrs Lazarus greeted them all with pleasure. 'I'm glad somebody doesn't want to give up yet!' Those lovely old blue eyes fixed themselves on Rebecca and sparkled for a moment. She recognized the visit for what it was: an expression of solidarity; a gesture. After all, there were only a few square yards left to dig and even the two students, who'd worked hard and well up to now, were lazing around. Jake was sitting on a rock strumming his guitar while Thomas brewed up some tea on a small camping stove. The whole atmosphere was one of the lethargy and listlessness.

But the six set to work with a will. A gesture it might be, and probably a hopeless one, but they only had an hour and they intended to make the most of it.

After they'd been working for a few minutes, to the pleasant sound of Jake's guitar, Mrs Lazarus — who was holding the metal detector quite close to where Rebecca was trowelling — suddenly turned her head.

'Sssh a minute, Jake. I think it's clicking.'

It was.

Charles Lazarus came over with a big spade and dug down, turning up some shovelfuls of spoil. He exchanged affectionate glances with his wife at the sight of the rapt expression on his mother's face. The truth was that the old detector often clicked like this, sometimes for no apparent reason. It wasn't very reliable. But his mother's indomitable spirit was an example to them all.

87

'Like to look through that lot, Rebecca?'

Delicately Rebecca riddled and sieved:

'I — I think there's something here,' she said at last, very solemnly.

It could be a coin. It was about the right size. It was completely encrusted with caked-on dirt. She started to scratch the dirt off with her finger nail, then it dropped off in one piece. They were all gathering round her.

'It *is* a coin!' she cried. 'It looks old!'

Clifford Johnson snatched it away from her, polishing it carefully in a soft cloth. He produced a magnifying glass, cradled the coin in the palm of his hand and looked.

'Good grief!'

His face rarely lit up but it now was quite animated. He looked slightly dazed.

'Yes. This is the real thing. No doubt about it.'

The excitement was unbelievable.

Mrs Lazarus was highly elated but she remained calm, as though this were entirely to be expected.

'Can you ring your Director and tell him, Clifford?' she asked. 'I'm sure the Willoughbys will let you use the phone.' She nodded to the rough road that led out of the cove and up to Mulberry Castle. 'He'll be pleased.'

'Pleased? I should think he'll drop everything and drive down here straight away! Oh, Charles,' he turned to Doctor Lazarus, 'I'm sorry I've been such a doubting Thomas, about your work on this. And Lottie — I'm sorry, Lottie.'

'And so you should be.' She caught Rebecca's eye and smiled. 'Shouldn't he?'

'Woof!' barked Blackie and Rebecca laughed.

'Cabro lives!' pronounced Sue.

It was all gloriously exciting.

As the six friends hurried around the headland to get

back to camp in time for the children's return, they skipped and danced beside the waves. Everything was turning out so well! Rebecca's mood in particular was one of great joy.

It wasn't going to last.

11
Shock Upon Shock

The news of the find spread quickly round the camp and even Miss Peabody was fascinated by it. Rebecca told Tommy, as soon as the children got back from their pleasure trip. She broke into the long description of

Mulberry Island he was starting to give her, to give him the news. He whistled and gave a wide smile of delight.

He was even prepared to overlook the fact that an outing he'd been looking forward to would now be postponed.

Antonia Lazarus came over to the camp after lunch to tell him.

'I'm sorry, Tommy,' she said, taking him by the arm. 'I know we promised to take you out in the car this afternoon, but will tomorrow do instead?'

It seemed that Mr Johnson had been right about his Director. Sir Nicholas Klaus, who had personally authorised the grant for Mrs Lazarus's work in Mulberry Cove for the past two years — and had come to regret it — had reacted to the news with great excitement. He'd ordered the party to spend the rest of the day digging, in particular to excavate to a depth of ten feet around the spot where the first coin had been found. He'd asked Mr Johnson to book him into the Trebizon Bay Hotel for the night. He intended to set off from the Midlands by car immediately and would be with them on site by the end of the afternoon.

Tommy was excited and full of questions.

'Will he be cross if you don't find nuffing more today?'

'No, Tommy, of course he won't!' The young Mrs Lazarus was in a state of euphoria. 'Our case is as good as proven! You see the Romans never settled in this part of the west country. There's no other explanation for that coin being in the cove. Cabro came here, just as Lottie's always maintained! We're prepared to dig for years now, if necessary —'

'Will you get some more money now, Aunty An?'

'I'm sure we will!' She laughed again. 'I don't expect we'll need it, though. The rest of the coins can't be far away. Our calculations — Uncle Charlie's calculations — were spot on.'

'I bet Mr Johnson feels a big fool,' said Tommy, with a sly grin.

'I think he does a bit. But he's apologized. Handsomely.'

She crossed to speak to Miss Peabody, over by the camp fire.

'The Willoughbys are planning a little sherry party for Sir Nicholas at six o'clock this evening. Up at the castle. To celebrate our success. You've been so kind, letting the girls come over and help. Could you come? And the house mistress who's in charge of them here –'

'Miss Morgan?'

'Yes. My husband's mother particularly wanted her invited. Could you have a word with her?'

'We could come along together,' said Miss Peabody, with pleasure. Sherry parties at castles were a little outside her normal line of duty. She would never have wanted to go alone. 'Can you hold the fort here, Donald — just for an hour or so?'

Her assistant nodded.

'The principal will take you both in her car, I'm sure,' said Antonia Lazarus. Apparently the Willoughbys, who knew Miss Welbeck well, had already phoned her and she'd accepted.

'I don't think a sherry party is much in your line, Rebecca,' she said with her delicate smile, just before she left the camp, 'but we'll have our own way of saying thank you to you and your friends, you can be quite sure. Perhaps tomorrow.'

Rebecca smiled back. The mood of joy was still with her.

That afternoon, Rebecca and Elf had some shopping

to do in town. Miss Peabody gave them a list of things to get at the chemist's shop: the first aid box was running low. They also wanted to get some dog biscuits for Blackie. They were taking him with them, on a lead, just in case he took it into his head to dive across the road.

Tommy wanted to come, too, especially now his outing had been postponed. He'd been refused permission to go and see what was happening at the dig — 'You'll get in the way, you silly boy. They're going to be very busy this afternoon!' — and he didn't want to join in the organized activities with the other children.

'Oh, all right then, Tommy,' said Miss Peabody. 'Keep an eye on him, you two.'

So off they all went, wearing anoraks in case it rained.

As they walked along, Tommy became conscious of the knobbly binoculars in his pocket and scowled to himself, hating them more than ever. A heavy burden of guilt settled on his shoulders, only lifting when he saw some big oil tankers way out to sea, as they reached the top road. 'Cor! Look at them ships!'

It was a long walk to town. When they reached the outskirts, Tommy took Blackie on the lead. 'We're goin' to get some biscuits for you, boy!' he said. Then, turning to Rebecca: 'Can we get him a big juicy bone as well with loads uv meat on it?'

'We'll see if we've got any money left,' smiled Rebecca.

They dropped down into the town, with its steep, narrow main street and picturesque old shop frontages. It was crowded with people and traffic, cars and bicycles and buses all mixed up, as today was market day in Trebizon.

They shopped at the chemist, then bought some dog biscuits at another shop. Rebecca had a spare carrier bag with her and handed it to Tommy. She also gave him a pound.

'Blackie's in luck — we have got some money. Look, there's the butcher's, three doors along. Go and see if he'll sell you a bone. Mind you don't lose the change. We'll hang on to Blackie for you.'

Rebecca had seen a dazzling window display. She dragged Blackie over by the lead.

'Look at these swim suits, Elf. Come and see!'

Tommy went to find the butcher's shop. He was about to put the pound in his anorak pocket when his fingers touched the binoculars again; he withdrew his hand quickly, as if scalded. He suddenly felt like screaming. If Rebecca knew he still had them and hadn't sent them back, she'd kill him! He should have sent them back . . . he *should* have done!

He found the right shop and the butcher wrapped up a huge juicy bone for him and handed him his money back. 'It's all right, son. You can have it on the house.'

But Tommy was staring. He was looking out into the street, through the big plate glass window of the butcher's shop. 'Thanks, mister,' he said, automatically putting the wrapped up bone in his carrier bag.

'What are you staring at, lad? Never seen a bus before?'

It had stopped right outside the shop. Its destination was written on the side, the words dancing hypnotically in front of Tommy's eyes. It was Fate, it must be. Fate was putting him to the test. Telling him what he really ought to do . . .

Suddenly Tommy dived out of the shop; the bus was starting to move away. He managed to leap on board just in time. Then it accelerated and went roaring away down the hill.

'Woof!' barked Blackie, tugging on the lead. He'd seen Tommy dive out of the butcher's shop, carrying an interesting looking bag, and jump on the bus. 'Woof! Woof!'

'Shut up, Blackie!' said Rebecca. She and Elf were still engrossed in the swim suits.

'I like that blue one, with the white edging,' said Elf.

'So do I,' said Rebecca.

'You're lucky,' smiled Elf. 'It'd fit you!'

'What d'you mean lucky?' laughed Rebecca. 'It's twenty pounds.'

'Woof! Woof!' said Blackie, tugging and straining on the lead.

Rebecca dragged her eyes away from the shop window. 'What *is* it, Blackie?' she frowned.

She looked up and down the street to see what had excited him. She didn't even notice the bus, which had now reached the bottom of Trebizon High Street and was going round the corner out of sight. He seemed to be pulling towards the butcher's shop.

'Maybe he realizes Tommy's in there choosing a bone for him,' Elf giggled.

'Maybe he wants to help choose it!' added Rebecca. '*No*, Blackie!' They were getting nearer the shop now. 'Don't you know you can't go in there?'

'Dogs aren't allowed in butcher's shops –' said Elf.

'For *very* good reasons,' added Rebecca. 'We'll have to wait outside!'

But Blackie didn't seem to want to go in the shop. He suddenly sat down on the pavement, at the spot where he'd seen Tommy jump on the bus, panting eagerly with his tongue hanging out, looking up and down the street.

'Thirsty?' inquired Rebecca.

Blackie got to his feet and started barking again.

There was a bus coming slowly down the High Street. It was a different bus, but Blackie wasn't to know that.

'Woof! Woof! *Woof!*'

Suddenly, to Rebecca's horror, he shot off the pavement with such force that the lead jerked out of her hand. '*Blackie!*' she shrieked. He was racing straight into a stream of traffic that was crawling down the hill. '*Blackie — come back this minute!*'

Blackie was weaving through the traffic and streaking towards the bus.

A car driver swerved to avoid him. There was a scream of brakes and then — bump! The car behind rammed his bumper. All the way up the hill brakes screamed on and cars banged in to each other.

Blackie, oblivious of the trail of disaster he was leaving, had now reached the bus and was trying to scramble on to the platform. 'Oh, no you don't!' A passenger caught him firmly by the collar. 'Whose blamed dog is this, anyway?'

Puffing for breath, Rebecca reached the platform and grabbed hold of Blackie's lead.

'You *bad* dog,' she said, her cheeks very red.

In the High Street, people were emerging from their cars, doors were slamming, damage was being inspected and voices were becoming shrill. A crowd gathered and then a policeman appeared.

'This is a fine mess,' he told Rebecca. She was holding on to Blackie firmly now. 'That your dog?' He took down all the details of the incident in a notebook. Fortunately nobody had been hurt, but minor dents and scratches on several cars were going to cost a lot to put right.

The policeman's car was parked nearby. At last he snapped his notebook shut:

'If you two young ladies would like to step this way,

with your dog, I'd better drive you back to your camp and report this.'

Rebecca's heart sunk. Elf was looking around anxiously.

'Where's Tommy?' she said. 'We're supposed to have a little boy with us,' she told the policeman.

'Oh?' he replied.

The butcher had come out of his shop and was standing on the pavement in his striped apron.

Rebecca questioned him urgently and he said: 'I gave the lad his bone and then he jumped on a bus.'

'On a *bus*?' exclaimed Rebecca. They both looked at Blackie. So that was it!

The policeman questioned the butcher quietly. Then he escorted the girls and Blackie to his car.

'It's all right, we'll catch him up at Battenbury.'

'Battenbury — ?' exclaimed Rebecca.

'Yes, lucky for us Mr Curtis noticed which bus it was. It was a green 'un with Battenbury Nature Park written up on the side.'

'Why on earth should Tommy have done that?' whispered Elf to Rebecca, in despair. 'Given us the slip and jumped on a bus to the nature park?'

'I suppose he just felt like it!' Rebecca whispered back, in fury.

But a few minutes' later, she found out the real reason.

The bus had got to Battenbury ahead of them and disgorged all its passengers outside the big ornamental gates to the nature park. As the policeman pulled up behind the bus, Blackie stuck his head out of the car window and started to bark.

Tommy was standing with his back to the gates, idly swinging the bag with the big bone in it.

He didn't notice the car, or Blackie barking at him.

He looked blissfully happy. He looked like a small boy who had just had a great weight lifted from his shoulders.

'Tommy!'

Rebecca, Elf and Blackie tumbled out of the car and ran towards him.

'What are you doing *here*, Tommy? Come *on*!'

In startled surprise he turned round and stared at them. 'Hey — did you follow me —?' he began.

Suddenly a woman standing by the gates shouted:

'You've left your binoculars behind, sonny.'

She came across with them. Tommy's face turned a deep beetroot red.

'They ain't mine,' he jerked out, then turned his back on her.

'I think they must belong to the nature park,' Rebecca said quickly. 'Perhaps you ought to hand them in at the ticket office.'

'Yes — yes, I will. Sorry. I thought the little boy left them by the gate.'

The woman took the binoculars away and handed them to an official, who smiled and thanked her.

The girls bundled Tommy into the back of the police car and then they were all driven back to camp.

Miss Peabody was just getting ready to go to the sherry party at Mulberry Castle when the police car brought them back. It was strange to see her in a dress instead of the usual white overall and ex-army trousers. When a crowd of children came running to her tent to tell her that a policeman had arrived with Blackie and Tommy Carter, she appeared in a trice, still holding her lipstick.

'*Now* what, Tommy?'

The policeman explained what.

Miss Peabody was very decisive about it all.

'The dog's a stray. I let the kids keep him at the camp against my better judgement. He'll have to go now. Can you take him down to the police station with you — ?'

'No!' screamed Tommy, falling on his knees beside Blackie and hugging him round the neck. 'Not yet! Don't send him away yet!' He stared up at Miss Peabody, tears running down his face. 'We just bought a lotta food for him! Look — we gotta big bone for him.' The dog was snuffling at the bag eagerly, trying to get the bone out. 'Not yet! Please, miss!'

Rebecca felt a deep, miserable ache. Tish, Sue, all of them were crowding round now, white-faced. They were willing Miss Peabody to take pity. There was a deathly hush and she could feel the weight of their stares. Even the policeman was shifting from one foot to the other, uneasily.

'All right, Tommy,' said Miss Peabody. 'You can keep him at camp one more night. We'll take him down to the police station in the morning, together.'

The officer nodded.

'Right. See you in the morning then, ma'am. 'Tis the best way. We'll try and find a proper home for 'ee. We'll do our best.'

The policeman drove away from the back of Juniper House. The crowd dispersed. Tommy led Blackie away to the tent, to give him his bone. Tish came and stood by Rebecca, putting an arm round her shoulders.

'What a horrible shock,' she said.

'Yes,' replied Rebecca, dully. She explained in full what had happened. 'Tommy had the binoculars all along! He decided to do the right thing at last — and this had to happen! And poor Blackie. He jerked the lead right out of my hand, but he was only trying to tell us that Tommy had jumped on a bus. He was trying to find him . . .'

Her eyes filled with tears.

'It's a shock,' Tish repeated.

But there was an even greater shock to come.

'You won't believe this, Rebecca.'

'The most awful thing's happened —'

'*What*?' demanded Rebecca. '*What's* happened?'

She was shaken. The other five had come to look for her and she could tell by their faces it was serious.

She'd just put Tommy to bed in the tent, comforting him for a long time because Blackie was leaving in the morning. Now she was sitting outside the tent, watching Blackie gnaw his big bone, listening out for Tommy in case he started crying again.

'What?' she repeated, looking up at the five solemn faces, then getting to her feet. 'Come on, tell me.'

'Miss Peabody's just got back from the party —'

'We overheard her talking to Donald. We heard everything. We couldn't help it —'

'Heard *what*?' begged Rebecca.

'Lottie's collapsed! She's in a state of shock!'

'She's in her room — under sedation for the night.'

'It's all because she's been found out!'

'What do you mean, *found out*?' cried Rebecca.

'The coin you found — Lottie planted it there herself.'

'*What*?' gasped Rebecca.

'It *is* a Roman coin of the right date,' Tish explained miserably. 'It's just that — it's one Lottie brought with her. From some other site. She well — sort of — faked the whole thing. Made sure you found it this morning, Rebeck.'

'But Sir Thing twigged what she'd done,' butted in Elf. 'There was a terrible row — and then Lottie collapsed. I suppose it was the disgrace of it all.'

Rebecca felt peculiar, as though she wanted to be sick.

'What — what's going to happen now?'

'Sir Thing almost had a heart attack himself apparently,' said Margot. 'He's told them to pack up the site in the morning. It's all finished.'

Pack up the site in the morning! First Blackie in disgrace — now Lottie.

Rebecca asked questions. How had the faking been discovered?

Apparently, in high spirits at the party, Charles Lazarus had taken Sir Nicholas Klaus up to his mother's room to show him the coin in her collection that came from the same mint as the one they'd now found. But the coin was missing!

When they'd come back to the party and questioned old Mrs Lazarus she'd gone into a state of shock and passed out. Then she'd been confused and rambling and they'd put her to bed under sedation.

Close examination revealed beyond any doubt that the coin missing from the collection and the coin found buried in the sand this morning were one and the same coin!

Miss Peabody had regaled Donald with the drama of it all and the five of them had listened in to the whole story.

'And everyone thinks Lottie was the person who planted the coin?' Rebecca asked at last, speaking slowly and deliberately. 'You, too?'

There was an embarrassed silence, broken by Tish.

'Who else could have done it, Rebeck? Charlie might have been a possibility — but it was him who discovered his mother's coin was missing! So it can't be him.'

'It had to be Lottie,' added Sue.

'She was just so sure she was right,' said Tish softly.

101

'She had to prove it somehow, didn't she?'

Mara looked troubled.

'What does Rebecca think?' she asked.

'I just think I'll go to bed,' replied Rebecca. She could hear movements inside the tent. 'I don't think Tommy's going to go to sleep tonight unless I do.'

now, warm enough to leave the tent flap open. Even Blackie dozed, curled up at Tommy's feet, guarding his bone.

Only Rebecca lay awake.

She lay and looked at the stars.

She could hear all the tiny night sounds. The others breathing in the tent; the distant thump and hiss of the waves breaking on the shore in Trebizon Bay; the crickets chirping; the hooting of an owl. Then she heard a nightingale, such a sweet sound that it made her feel sadder than ever.

She closed her eyes, alone with her night thoughts.

Poor Tommy! Soon to be cast adrift again. No Blackie. No 'Uncle Charlie' and 'Aunty An'. She thought about her uncomfortable feeling in the garden of the empty house in Bath and shivered slightly. But she was all right. She had marvellous friends! And she'd be seeing Mum and Dad soon!

Poor Blackie, too. What would become of him? Rebecca didn't like to think about that too deeply. Would the police really be able to find a good home for a large scruffy mongrel dog with an expensive appetite?

And poor, poor Mrs Lazarus!

How bad was she? Would she be all right again by morning?

After all, she was an old lady.

She remembered being in the cove, at sunset that evening, the eerie voice declaiming from a cave, in Latin. Mrs Lazarus, communing with the past — with Cabro! *One can't help feeling a certain affection for him!*

And then she'd said:

Proof of his misdeeds is hidden right here in this cove!

Proof . . . misdeeds . . . Tommy Carter. Rebecca was getting muddled and sleepy.

104

I think it's quite conclusive but some people think I'm dotty. Dotty Lottie!

Dotty Lottie.

They'd think she was dottier than ever, after this.

Now in a cave in a distant cove lies the hero's prize, sleeping like the lion.

She wasn't dotty! Of course she wasn't.

She didn't plant that coin. She wouldn't do a thing like that.

But if *she* didn't . . . then who did?

Who?

Who, who, who?

'Whoo — Whoo — Whoo?' replied the owl.

Rebecca was asleep.

Antonia Lazarus was wide awake. Up at Mulberry Castle, she lay in bed, pleading with her husband.

'Charles.'

'Toni, don't keep on about the boy. I'm tired.'

'But we were going to have a chat with Sheila Peabody before we left. You know we were.'

'Look, Toni, only one thing matters at the moment. That's to get mother home in the morning. It's all been too much of a strain for her. We've got to get her away from here quickly, so she can get Cabro out of her head.'

His voice was weary and full of his own dazed disappointment.

'I must get him out of my head, too. Try to abandon him.'

'But we're not going to abandon Tommy, as well?' his wife whispered. 'Not now we've found him?'

'I don't know,' said Doctor Lazarus. 'All I do know is that I'm in no state to make a decision.'

105

12
The Message in the Bottle

As though comforted by her presence, Tommy fell asleep very soon after Rebecca came to bed. It wasn't long before Elf crawled into the tent, climbed into her sleeping bag and fell asleep, too. It was a warm night now, warm enough to leave the tent flap open. Even Blackie dozed, curled up at Tommy's feet, guarding his bone.

Only Rebecca lay awake.

She lay and looked at the stars.

She could hear all the tiny night sounds. The others breathing in the tent; the distant thump and hiss of the waves breaking on the shore in Trebizon Bay; the crickets chirping; the hooting of an owl. Then she heard a nightingale, such a sweet sound that it made her feel sadder than ever.

She closed her eyes, alone with her night thoughts.

Poor Tommy! Soon to be cast adrift again. No Blackie. No 'Uncle Charlie' and 'Aunty An'. She thought about her uncomfortable feeling in the garden of the empty house in Bath and shivered slightly. But she was all right. She had marvellous friends! And she'd be seeing Mum and Dad soon!

Poor Blackie, too. What would become of him? Rebecca didn't like to think about that too deeply. Would the police really be able to find a good home for a large scruffy mongrel dog with an expensive appetite?

And poor, poor Mrs Lazarus!

How bad was she? Would she be all right again by morning?

After all, she was an old lady.

She remembered being in the cove, at sunset that evening, the eerie voice declaiming from a cave, in Latin. Mrs Lazarus, communing with the past — with Cabro! *One can't help feeling a certain affection for him*!

And then she'd said:

Proof of his misdeeds is hidden right here in this cove!

Proof . . . misdeeds . . . Tommy Carter. Rebecca was getting muddled and sleepy.

I think it's quite conclusive but some people think I'm dotty. Dotty Lottie!

Dotty Lottie.

They'd think she was dottier than ever, after this.

Now in a cave in a distant cove lies the hero's prize, sleeping like the lion.

She wasn't dotty! Of course she wasn't.

She didn't plant that coin. She wouldn't do a thing like that.

But if *she* didn't . . . then who did?

Who?

Who, who, who?

'Whoo — Whoo — Whoo?' replied the owl.

Rebecca was asleep.

Antonia Lazarus was wide awake. Up at Mulberry Castle, she lay in bed, pleading with her husband.

'Charles.'

'Toni, don't keep on about the boy. I'm tired.'

'But we were going to have a chat with Sheila Peabody before we left. You know we were.'

'Look, Toni, only one thing matters at the moment. That's to get mother home in the morning. It's all been too much of a strain for her. We've got to get her away from here quickly, so she can get Cabro out of her head.'

His voice was weary and full of his own dazed disappointment.

'I must get him out of my head, too. Try to abandon him.'

'But we're not going to abandon Tommy, as well?' his wife whispered. 'Not now we've found him?'

'I don't know,' said Doctor Lazarus. 'All I do know is that I'm in no state to make a decision.'

Rebecca awoke at first light. She wriggled up into sitting position and then unzipped her sleeping bag and peered around. There was something different about the tent.

Then she realised. She shook Elf awake, urgently.

'Uh?'

'Tommy's gone!'

She pulled back the tent flap as far as it would go, to let in more of the grey dawn light. She peered round the tent again. Not only had Tommy gone, but so had his sleeping bag and small bag. So had Blackie. And so had Blackie's big bone.

'Quick, Elf!' she whispered. 'We'd better get after them.'

She realised that it might have been the slight sounds and movements of a stealthy departure that had caused her to wake so early. They couldn't have got far!

They scrambled into their clothes as quickly as they could, then ducked out of the tent.

The entire camp lay sleeping. The sun wasn't even peeping up yet.

'Look!' whispered Rebecca, pointing down the track that led towards the wicket gate. Some socks had dropped out of Tommy's bag. 'They went that way.'

Silently, on tip-toe, the two girls ran down the track, past the camp fire, and out through the little gate. They ran up and over the dunes and out on the flat expanse of sand. The tide was a long way out. Right down to the waves' edge the sand lay smooth and clean – or almost –

'Look, footprints!' exclaimed Elf.

'And paw prints!' added Rebecca, bending down to look.

'Come on, Elf!'

They raced across the sands, following the tracks.

'They – they just seem to lead straight down to the

106

water's edge,' gasped Elf, puffing to keep up with Rebecca. 'Surely they can't have gone for a swim?'

At last they reached the shore. The prints seemed to have come to a full stop.

Rebecca gazed out at the great empty sea, heart thumping with fear, but suddenly Elf cried:

'It's all right – they carry on again here. They walked along the shore.'

'Thank goodness for that,' began Rebecca, turning and following Elf. Then she stared down at her feet. 'Hey, Elf. Look at this!'

A bottle was bobbing up and down, right by the shore. She reached out and grabbed it.

'It's got a piece of paper rolled up in it!'

Elf ran back to her side, her eyes wide with interest. 'A message in a bottle!'

'I think it must be from Tommy,' said Rebecca. 'I think that's why he headed straight for the water – to throw the bottle in first – before going off somewhere.'

It was a screw top bottle. She took the top off and then very carefully withdrew a piece of paper. There was a message written in wobbly capital letters. –

WEN YOU READ THIS ME AND BLACKIE WILL BE IN OUR NEW HOUSE. NOBODY WILL NEVER FIND US. PLEESE TELL THEM LOTTIE NEVER DONE IT. IT WAS ME. THIS IS MY CONFESHION AND I AM TRULEY SORRY. SIGNED TOMMY CARTER AGE 8.

Rebecca and Elf read the message through twice. Then they stared at each other.

'It wasn't Lottie!' began Elf.

Rebecca nodded. She wanted to shout it out with relief.

'The coin! It was Tommy!'

'The little wretch!' exclaimed Elf, in amazement. 'He must have broken into the castle then!'

'He's broken in before!' cried Rebecca. '*And* he knew about the coin! Oh, how stupid of me not to remember that.'

'But to go to all the trouble!'

'He wanted to help Uncle Charlie!' Rebecca realised. 'He was upset because Mr Johnson had said the calculations were all wrong — don't you remember how quiet he was the other afternoon, after some squabble?'

They were walking along the shore now, into the dawn, following the footprints again.

'Of course,' nodded Elf. 'He wanted to prove Charlie's calculations were right! So he must have bunked over to Mulberry Castle that evening and got the coin, then buried it in the sand last thing . . .'

'And I found it the next morning! Yesterday morning!'

Suddenly Rebecca remembered Tommy grinning slyly at Antonia Lazarus — *I bet Mr Johnson feels a big fool*.

But right now only one thing mattered to Rebecca.

'This is going to make Lottie feel tons better! Oh, poor thing — what a nightmare for her! First of all the dreadful shock that it wasn't Cabro after all. And then everyone thinking — Sir Nicholas thinking — it was *her* who planted it. That was the *real* shock.'

'And maybe she began to wonder if she'd gone mad or something!' Elf pointed out. 'After all, nobody but her *could* have done it and yet at the same time she knew she *hadn't* done it.'

'I can't wait to tell her!' exclaimed Rebecca. 'I just can't wait!'

The footprints beside the shore were leading them right round the headland now, towards Mulberry Cove.

'I wonder where he's gone?' mused Elf.

'Oh, he can't be far away,' said Rebecca. She looked at the message again. 'He's going to make a house for him and Blackie. What's the betting he found a good cave round in Mulberry sometime? Oh, *poor* Tommy.'

They were both very quiet as they clambered over the slippery rocks covered in bladderwrack that led round into the cove at low tide. They were thinking about Tommy — and Blackie. Blackie was going to be taken away from him this morning. 'Seems almost cruel to find them and bring them back, doesn't it?' observed Elf, at last.

'Yes,' said Rebecca, sadly.

At last they could see round into the cove. It was eerie and shadowy in the early silvery-grey light. They shaded their eyes and scanned the beach for some sight of the boy and the dog. And then suddenly Rebecca gasped.

'Look, Elf!'

A sailing boat had slid out from behind some rocks, its sail filled with breeze. It was just leaving the sheltered waters of the cove and entering the rough water of the open sea, and it was starting to switchback up and down.

It appeared to be trying to head in the direction of Mulberry Island.

13
The Riddle is Solved

'Tommy!' screamed Rebecca.

But he probably couldn't hear and even if he could, there wasn't much he could do about it. He'd lost hold of the mainsheet. The little sailing dinghy was out of his control now, tossing up and down on the waves, flinging boy, dog, sleeping bag and luggage first to one side and then to the other.

'Can't we get help?' cried Elf.

'There isn't time. Come on — let's run!'

They raced pell mell up the beach to the sailing hut. Rebecca heaved open the lid of the lifejacket chest and threw one over to Elf. 'Quick, put it on!'

Elf heaved a lifebelt off its hook and bounced it into the nearest sailing dinghy, which was on a launching trolley.

They heaved and pushed the trolley all the way down the beach as fast as they could go and then launched the dinghy into shallow water. They waded through the cold surf and clambered on board the boat; they were both wearing their lifejackets now.

'You start rowing, while I get the mainsail up — it'll give us a bit of speed,' said Rebecca, her fingers trembling as she untied knots. 'Is Tommy still the right way up?'

'Yes,' said Elf, glancing over her shoulder as she heaved on the oars. 'Don't know how.'

First the mainsail and then the jibsail filled with breeze and the little dinghy started to whip along in the cove, heading for the open sea. Elf was able to ship the oars. 'We're making good speed now,' said Rebecca in relief, holding the tiller and the mainsheet. 'Got the jibsheet, Elf? All you have to do is hang on and do what I say.'

They would have felt frightened, but there was too much to do.

Out on the open sea, Tommy felt very frightened.

It had seemed such an adventure at first, setting sail with Blackie. He'd watched the older children have sailing lessons in the cove and he was sure he knew exactly what to do. He'd made quite a good job of launching the boat and letting out the mainsail. They were off!

They were heading for Mulberry Island! Their own island — their very own kingdom. And it even had a house on it, too. There were fruit and vegetables to pinch from the garden, growing amongst the weeds and nettles, because he'd seen them. They'd live there forever, him and Blackie, and nobody would ever find them. Nobody could try and mess them around, ever again.

He didn't like the proper world, anyway. Everything you did seemed to turn out wrong.

They were going to make a fresh start in life, just the two of them!

But as soon as the dinghy hit the open sea, his excitement faded. The wind was much stronger and the waves much bigger. The mainsheet was jerked out of his hand and the mainsail began to flap noisily, the boom swinging backwards and forwards and nearly knocking him out of the boat each time. Then he lost hold of the tiller, too, as big waves reared up and the boat seemed almost to stand on end. Soon he was drenched from head to foot and felt seasick, thrown about the boat as it tossed and pitched.

Blackie cowered in the bottom of the boat, his coat dripping with salt water, whining with fear.

Then Tommy realised he hadn't put on one of those orange things, lifejacket things, and he became more frightened than ever. They weren't going to make it! They'd never get to Mulberry Island at this rate!

The only thing for it was to try and get hold of the mainsheet again, and then the tiller, turn the boat right round and head straight back to Mulberry Cove.

Gasping and panting he lay in the bottom of the boat, the spray washing over him from every direction, trying to get hold of the slippery rope. At the third attempt, he got it and hung on to it tight as he crawled back to the tiller.

He felt the mainsheet go taut in his hand as the mainsail stopped flapping and filled with wind; he held on fast, turned and grabbed the tiller. Now, if he pulled the tiller hard over, the rudder would work and the boat would go round in a full circle . . .

It was turning . . . turning . . . It was easy! Like driving a car at the dodgems! Soon they'd be facing the other way, heading straight back to Mulberry Cove —

He thought he could hear a voice shouting, carried on the wind.

'No, Tommy! Take the tiller back. You'll gybe! *Take it back!*'

A sailing boat was bearing down on him — a voice was calling —

Suddenly, with a great crash, the world turned upside down. He was heeling over backwards, into the sea.

'He's capsized!' screamed Elf.

In her room at Mulberry Castle, Mrs Lottie Lazarus had woken at dawn. She felt horrible; as if she'd been drugged. She felt as though she'd been having bad dreams. She struggled into a sitting position and gradually her head cleared. The events of the previous evening came back to her.

She got out of bed and washed her face in cold water at the hand basin, several times.

She dried her face on a towel and decided to get dressed.

'What a nonsense!' she thought. 'Letting myself go

113

under like that. Who played that damnfool trick? We've got two more days — and we've still got a patch to dig. If Nick thinks we're going home today, he's got another think coming.'

As soon as she'd dressed, she walked across to her window, drew the curtains back and gazed out. High up in the castle here, she had a bird's eye view of the cove. She looked down at it, the sands newly-washed.

'Oh, Cabro,' she murmured. 'How you must be laughing. *You* know where it is, don't you?'

She lifted her head slightly and looked across to Mulberry Island, a silhouette against a sky streaked with purple and silver. It was a beautiful sunrise.

Then she scanned the sea for a while. Her eyes widened.

Two minutes later she was hammering feverishly at her son's bedroom door.

He came to the door and found his mother standing there, a wild look about her.

'Get the Range Rover out, Charles. We're going straight down to the cove.'

He took her by the arm.

'No, mother,' he said gently. 'You're not going down to the cove, ever again. Come on, I'm taking you back to bed.'

She jerked her arm free.

'Don't be so stupid, Charles,' she said. 'A boat's capsized. I think someone may be drowning.'

Blackie had the advantage over Tommy. He could swim. Valiantly the dog struggled through the water and Rebecca helped him on board.

Then he shook himself several times and barked in Tommy's direction.

Rebecca was holding the boat steady, keeping it on an

even keel. Elf was yelling at Tommy.

'Grab it, Tommy! Just grab hold if it! We'll haul you in!' She had thrown him the lifebelt.

But Tommy didn't seem to hear. He was stubbornly clinging on to the side of the upturned dinghy but the waves kept battering at him. He was swallowing salt water – mouthfuls of it.

Then a huge wave washed over him, and he lost his grip.

'He's going under!' cried Rebecca, in terror. 'Elf! Be careful!'

Elf had jumped over the side, her lifejacket inflated. 'I'll get him!'

Rebecca sat there, almost paralysed with fear. There was nothing she could do to help. Somebody had to keep the boat steady, or they'd all be drowned! Elf was a strong swimmer, but the waves seemed like mountains this morning. She'd got the lifeline tied round her waist, attached to the lifebelt as she swam.

She grabbed Tommy as he bobbed up to the surface for the second time and got his legs through the lifebelt. Then she hooked his arms over either side, before his small frame could slide straight through it. She struggled back towards the dinghy, towing Tommy behind her.

Once or twice a big wave obliterated her from view and Rebecca would cry: 'Elf? Elf?' But she made it. As she pulled herself back into the boat, the lifeline still tied round her waist, Rebecca was trembling. Together, at the third attempt, they managed to lift Tommy into the dinghy and the boat dipped down, terrifyingly. Then it straightened up.

'Let's get him back to shore, quickly,' said Rebecca. Fighting down a feeling of panic, she brought the boat about skilfully in the tossing waters, just as she'd been taught.

Then they were tacking back to the cove. Soon they were passing by the rock of the lion and were in sheltered waters again.

For a while Tommy lay moaning in the bottom of the boat, while Elf pumped him and Blackie stood guard.

Then the little boy started to be sick and they knew he was all right.

'There's a white range rover coming down the beach,' said Elf. She was shivering now.

'It's the Lazaruses!' exclaimed Rebecca.

As they came into shore, people waded out and pulled the dinghy in the last few yards.

Doctor Lazarus lifted Tommy out and carried him in his arms.

Jake helped the two girls ashore and Mrs Lottie Lazarus came forward with warm blankets for them. They wrapped up in them, gratefully, their teeth chattering.

Rebecca was relieved to see Mrs Lazarus, up and about so early, apparently fully recovered.

'The — the coin,' she shivered. 'It — it was Tommy! T-Tommy put it there!'

'Tommy?' It took a moment for the news to sink in. 'Oh, the little rogue!'

Doctor Lazarus was attending to Tommy. He'd wrapped him up in a thick blanket and was sitting on a rock cradling him in his arms. The little boy looked up at him and smiled. 'All right Tommy?' he asked.

'I bin a nuisance,' said Tommy. He closed his eyes. 'Ain't I?'

When Mrs Lazarus came up beside them, her son was gazing down tenderly into the pale face of the little boy.

'He's like Paul, isn't he, mother?' he said.

116

'Of course he's not like Paul,' she snorted. 'Dear little Paul was always very correct!' Suddenly she smiled. She looked up the cove towards the excavations. 'He's altogether much more like Cabro — wretched Cabro!'

Cabro.

At the mention of that name, a shadow crossed the doctor's face, but his mother returned her gaze to Tommy. She was still smiling. 'It would be rather lovely to have a grandchild again, and I daresay you could keep him on the straight and narrow, Charles.'

'What's the matter with Blackie?' asked Rebecca. 'He seems to be gnawing an imaginary bone.'

'He buried the bone,' said Tommy.

'He's been doing that gnawing business for ages,' laughed Elf. 'I expect he's got something stuck in his teeth again!'

It was amazing how quickly they had recovered from their ordeal. The wind had dropped and the sun was coming up now, filling the cove with warmth. It was going to be a hot day. They sat on the rocks, wrapped in the blankets. Antonia Lazarus had appeared with flasks of hot soup for them. Jake had gone to the camp to see if Miss Peabody was up yet, although it was still very early. She might be anxious if she discovered that their tent was empty.

After that he was going to get some men and a motor boat and organize the towing in of the capsized sailing dinghy. It was still bobbing around on the open sea.

'Oh, do stop it, Blackie,' smiled Rebecca.

He was still chewing and pawing at his mouth.

'We need Tish,' said Elf. 'She knows how to get things out of his mouth.'

'Here, let me try,' said Charles Lazarus. 'Come here, boy.'

He took hold of the dog's jaws and prised them open, so the teeth were bared.

He felt around and then got hold of something between finger and thumb and pulled.

'It's wedged solid. Ah. Here it comes.'

He held the small object up. It was round. It glittered like gold in the sun's rays.

It *was* gold.

They all stared.

Lottie Lazarus held out her hand. She was trembling.

'Charles. What is it? Let me see.'

He was cradling it in the palm of his hand, examining it closely. Then he handed it to his mother and she looked at it, too. Very closely. The silence amongst them all was electric. Rebecca could actually hear her heart beating.

'Is it —?' she asked.

But there was no need to ask. The look on Lottie's face provided the answer. Elation; jubilation; incredulous joy. It was a Roman coin of the third century, A.D. One of Cabro's hoard.

Blackie barked and wagged his tail.

'Where did you *get* it, boy?' gasped Antonia Lazarus.

'Tell us, boy, tell us!' pleaded Tommy.

Blackie just barked unintelligibly.

Suddenly Rebecca said:

'What did you say about him burying the bone, Tommy? When? Where did he bury it?'

'We brought it wiv us,' said Tommy, slowly. 'I wanted him to have it in our new house. But he buried it first. Before we got in the boat.'

'Here, in the cove?' said Rebecca eagerly. The three Lazaruses exchanged looks.

Everyone was on their feet.

'Come on, Blackie!' shouted Tommy, leading the way up the beach. 'Come and show 'em!'

The dog ran beside him. When Tommy got roughly to the spot, he said: 'Bone! Find yer bone!'

Blackie sniffed around for a while. Everybody held their breath in suspense. Then he selected a spot and started to dig. He dug down until he found the bone, tugged it out and then ran off across the beach with it, holding it in his mouth.

Lottie Lazarus sunk down on her knees at the spot where the bone had been. She scrabbled in the sand with her bare hands.

'The treasure!' gasped Tommy. She was bringing up coins, from a broken pot. They were dripping through her fingers.

'Cabro!' she cried. 'You scoundrel. Now, at last, history can be rewritten!'

It seemed to Rebecca for a moment that time stood still and the wily old Roman was here in the cove once more. Down on her knees, Mrs Lazarus began to laugh. She was in the lea of the cliffs, the early morning sun throwing a long pointed shadow beside her. She was laughing with joy.

Suddenly from the nearby caves, the laughter came echoing back.

The riddle was solved. The misappropriated funds of eighteen hundred years ago would now, no doubt, be dealt with correctly and worthily by appropriate people. The 'hero's prize' lay sleeping no longer. It had been found.

But not inside the area that had been staked off.

It was outside it, by a mere two yards.

14
Going Home

After that, Charles and Antonia Lazarus wouldn't hear of Blackie being taken into police custody.

They wanted to keep him.

They also wanted to keep Tommy.

Miss Peabody telephoned London and dealt with the official side of things and within 24 hours it was confirmed. Doctor and Mrs Lazarus would be allowed to take Tommy home with them, straight after camp, for a trial fostering period. If things worked out, the fostering arrangement would be permanent.

Everybody was quite sure that things would work out. Because, for the first time in his life, Tommy wanted them to. He was planning to be good — well, reasonably good! — and besides he had Blackie to think about now. He wasn't going to mess things up for him and Blackie, not if he could help it!

Rebecca and Elf had to recount the story to the other four, in much detail. Several times.

Frustrated at missing such excitement, such high drama, they now contented themselves by reliving it at secondhand. 'To think us four were all fast asleep!' groaned Sue. At least they were allowed time off camp to go and watch the coins being brought out by experts, under the personal supervision of Sir Nicholas Klaus, who was now in a great state of euphoria.

'Elf was really brave,' Rebecca told Tish and Sue. 'The sea was rough, I can tell you. I was scared.'

'You did pretty well yourself then,' said Sue.

But they all loved Elf more than ever now. Tommy worshipped her. When the Lazaruses treated them all to an enormous cream tea at the Dennizon Point Hotel, Tommy tried to give Elf his chocolate eclairs. But even Elf couldn't manage them.

The camp ended with two very hot days and plenty of swimming in the sea. In the evenings Rebecca got back to some tennis. Miss Willis insisted upon it and played singles with her on the staff court. 'You've got your first tennis competition next week — Frinton, isn't it?'

On the Saturday morning, camp ended. All the tents

and equipment were packed up and loaded back on to the big lorry that had brought them down to Trebizon in the first place. By mid-day the site was cleared and the little copse behind Juniper House was back to normal, the only difference being a blackened patch in the clearing, where the camp fire had been.

There were lots of good-byes as the Trebizon volunteers parted company with the children who'd been in their charge for a whole fortnight. Some of the good-byes were very tearful, with hugs and kisses and swapping of names and addresses and promises to write.

After the children had gone, the six felt sad and ran over to Court House to take their minds off it.

'Let's try and get in and see what rooms we want!' said Margot.

'They're different upstairs, aren't they,' added Sue.

'There are three twos, one four and two singles. We can't be in threes again,' contemplated Mara. She looked at Tish and smiled. 'Perhaps we should all have a change around in the Fourth Year?'

Sue wasn't too sure how she felt about that. Margot and Elf just smiled at each other and shrugged.

Tish rattled at the front door. But the Barringtons were still away on holiday and the entire building was locked. Their trunks had long since been removed and were waiting for them at Juniper House.

'Looks as though we'll just have to wait and see next term,' said Rebecca. 'Wonder if Tish will be head of games next term?'

'You still haven't decided your options, Rebeck!' said Tish, changing the subject.

'How do you know?' smiled Rebecca. And then, as a yellow car scrunched into the forecourt of Court House, she let out a cry: —

'It's Mum and Dad! They're early!'

'Rebecca!' exclaimed her father, as both her parents stepped out of the hired car. 'Miss Morgan thought you might be over here.'

She fell into their arms.

'It's been so long, hasn't it, Becky!' said Mrs Mason, rather tearful as she embraced her. 'You've grown! You've grown!'

Too long, thought Rebecca. Much too long!

They'd bought her a lovely birthday present. A tiny silver locket, engraved with her initials.

When they all got back to Juniper House, the Lazaruses had come to say good-bye.

The big white Range Rover was packed with their luggage. Lottie was sitting in the back, very erect, with Tommy and Blackie; Doctor Lazarus was sitting at the steering wheel, his wife beside him. While the adults all talked for a while the six gathered round the open back of the vehicle and hugged Tommy and patted Blackie.

'Good-bye, Tommy. Good-bye, Blackie!' said Rebecca, feeling very emotional. She'd never forget them.

'Woof!' said the dog. He had seen a butterfly.

'Oh, Blackie, you've still got that old bone!' laughed Rebecca. 'Didn't it just bring us luck, Tommy! You thinking of buying him that bone!'

'I think I'd like to preserve it in aspic!' said Lottie Lazarus. She leaned forward in her seat and took Rebecca's young hands in her old ones. 'Now, Rebecca, I'd like you to kiss me good-bye. I'm sure we shall meet again some time.'

Rebecca kissed the weatherbeaten cheek and suddenly burst out, 'I've decided something! I couldn't decide what to do next year, but now I know. I'm going to learn some Latin. I think that's going to be really interesting!'

Mrs Lazarus merely expressed surprise. 'D'you mean to tell me that it isn't compulsory at Trebizon these days?'

When the Range Rover left, Rebecca and her parents were right behind it in the yellow car. Her trunk and tennis rackets were in the boot. They bumped along the narrow winding track that meandered through the school grounds, right on the tail of the other vehicle. Tish, Sue, Elf, Mara and Margot pelted along behind for a little way, puffing and waving and shouting, 'Bye, Rebeck; 'bye, see you next term!'

At the main gates, the vehicles parted company. The Range Rover went to the left and the yellow car went to the right. Rebecca and Tommy waved and waved to each other until each was out of sight.

Rebecca clasped her knees and stared out across the bay as her father whipped the car along the top road.

The summer camp was over. She'd be back at Trebizon soon — they'd be going into the Fourth next term!

But right now she was going home.

And so was Tommy.

Fiction in paperback from Dragon Books

Richard Dubleman

The Adventures of Holly Hobbie   £1.25   ☐

Anne Digby
Trebizon series

First Term at Trebizon	85p	☐
Second Term at Trebizon	95p	☐
Summer Term at Trebizon	85p	☐
Boy Trouble at Trebizon	95p	☐
More Trouble at Trebizon	95p	☐
The Tennis Term at Trebizon	95p	☐
Summer Camp at Trebizon	95p	☐
Into the Fourth at Trebizon	£1.25	☐
The Big Swim of the Summer	60p	☐

Elyne Mitchell

Silver Brumby's Kingdom	85p	☐
Silver Brumbies of the South	75p	☐
Silver Brumby	85p	☐
Silver Brumby's Daughter	85p	☐
Silver Brumby Whirlwind	50p	☐
Son of the Whirlwind	65p	☐
Moon Filly	60p	☐

Mary O'Hara

My Friend Flicka Part One	85p	☐
My Friend Flicka Part Two	85p	☐

To order direct from the publisher just tick the titles you want
and fill in the order form.

Fiction in paperback from Dragon Books

Peter Glidewell

Schoolgirl Chums	£1.25	☐
St Ursula's in Danger	£1.25	☐

Gerald Frow

Young Sherlock: The Mystery of the Manor House	95p	☐

Frank Richards

Billy Bunter of Greyfriars School	£1.25	☐
Billy Bunter's Double	£1.25	☐
Billy Bunter Comes for Christmas	£1.25	☐
Billy Bunter Does His Best	£1.25	☐

T R Burch

The Mercury Cup	£1.25	☐

Granville Wilson

War of the Computers	85p	☐

Marlene Fanta Shyer

My Brother the Thief	95p	☐

David Rees

Exeter Blitz	75p	☐

Anne Knowles

The Stirrup and the Ground	£1.25	☐

Erik Haugaard

Chase Me, Catch Nobody	£1.25	☐

Joan Lowery Nixon

The Spectre	£1.25	☐
The Séance	£1.25	☐

Caroline Akrill

Eventer's Dream	£1.50	☐
A Hoof in the Door	£1.50	☐
Ticket to Ride	£1.50	☐

To order direct from the publisher just tick the titles you want
and fill in the order form.

Fiction in paperback from Dragon Books

Ann Jungmann
Vlad the Drac   95p ☐

Thomas Meehan
Annie   £1.25 ☐

Michael Denton
Eggbox Brontosaurus   85p ☐

Marika Hanbury Tenison
The Princess and the Unicorn   £1.25 ☐

Alan Davidson
A Friend Like Annabel   £1.25 ☐
Just Like Annabel   £1.25 ☐

Felix Salten
Bambi's Children Part One   60p ☐
Bambi's Children Part Two   60p ☐

T R Burch
Ben and Blackbeard   £1.25 ☐
Ben on Coles Hill   £1.25 ☐

Jonathan Rumbold
The Adventures of Niko   £1.25 ☐

Marcus Crouch
The Ivory City   95p ☐

Lynne Reid Banks
The Indian in the Cupboard   £1.25 ☐
I, Houdini   £1.25 ☐

Nina Beachcroft
The Wishing People   £1.25 ☐
Well Met by Witchlight   £1.25 ☐
Under the Enchanter   £1.25 ☐
A Visit to Folly Castle   £1.25 ☐
A Spell of Sleep   £1.25 ☐
Cold Christmas   £1.25 ☐

Carol Adorjan
The Catsitter Mystery   £1.25 ☐

To order direct from the publisher just tick the titles you want and fill in the order form.

All these books are available at your local bookshop or newsagent, or can be ordered direct from the publisher.

To order direct from the publisher just tick the titles you want and fill in the form below.

Name _____

Address _____

_____

Send to:
Dragon Cash Sales
PO Box 11, Falmouth, Cornwall TR10 9EN.

Please enclose remittance to the value of the cover price plus:

UK 45p for the first book, 20p for the second book plus 14p per copy for each additional book ordered to a maximum charge of £1.63.

BFPO and Eire 45p for the first book, 20p for the second book plus 14p per copy for the next 7 books, thereafter 8p per book.

Overseas 75p for the first book and 21p for each additional book.

Dragon Books reserve the right to show new retail prices on covers, which may differ from those previously advertised in the text or elsewhere.